KT-552-959

MO O'HARA

ILLUSTRATED BY MAREK JAGUCKI

MACMILLAN CHILDREN'S BOOKS

First published 2014 by Macmillan Children's Books
a division of Macmillan Publishers Limited
20 New Wharf Road, London N1 9RR
Basingstoke and Oxford
Associated companies throughout the world
www.panmacmillan.com

ISBN 978-1-4472-6295-4

Text copyright © Mo O'Hara 2014
Illustrations copyright © Marek Jagucki 2014

The right of Mo O'Hara and Marek Jagucki to be identified as the author and illustrator of this work has been asserted by them in accordance with the Copyright, Designs and Patents Act 1988.

All rights reserved. No part of this publication may be reproduced, stored in or introduced into a retrieval system, or transmitted, in any form or by any means (electronic, mechanical, photocopying, recording or otherwise), without the prior written permission of the publisher. Any person who does any unauthorized act in relation to this publication may be liable to criminal prosecution and civil claims for damages.

1 3 5 7 9 8 6 4 2

A CIP catalogue record for this book is available from the British Library.

Printed and bound by CPI Group (UK) Ltd, Croydon CR0 4YY

This book is sold subject to the condition that it shall not, by way of trade or otherwise, be lent, resold, hired out, or otherwise circulated without the publisher's prior consent in any form of binding or cover other than that in which it is published and without a similar condition including this condition being imposed on the subsequent purchaser.

FIFE CULTURAL TRUST
FCT50484

WITHDRAWN FROM STOCK

MY BIG FAT ZOMBIE GOLDFISH

ANY FIN IS POSSIBLE

Mo O'Hara grew up in Pennsylvania, USA, but now lives in south-east London. She began her writing and acting career by touring theatres and schools across the UK and Ireland, working as a storyteller. As well as writing books for children Mo has written comedy sketches for Radio 4 and performed her own material in London and Edinburgh. Mo and her big brother once brought their own pet goldfish back from the brink of death.

Books by Mo O'Hara

My Big Fat Zombie Goldfish
My Big Fat Zombie Goldfish: The SeaQuel
My Big Fat Zombie Goldfish: Fins of Fury
My Big Fat Zombie Goldfish: Any Fin Is Possible

Quotes from* My Big Fat Zombie Goldfish *readers

'This Franktastic story was so much fun it blew my socks off!' **Sharif (aged 8)**

'I wish I had a swishy fishy!' **Robin (aged 7)**

'Don't look at Frankie! He'll zombify you and you won't be able to stop reading!' **Adil (aged 8)**

'*My Big Fat Zombie Goldfish* is a zombitastic book you won't be able to put down' **Leon (aged 9)**

'It's really funny and Frankie makes me laugh lots' **Spike (aged 7)**

'It was awesome. I read all day when I got it and I couldn't put it down until I was finished' **Becky (aged nearly 9)**

FIFE COUNCIL
WITHDRAWN FROM STOCK

50484	
PETERS	10-Feb-2015
JF	£5.99
JHUM	FIFE

To my mom and dad.
The best parents in the world.

THE CURSE OF THE CAT OF KINGS

CHAPTER 1

THE LEGEND BEGINS

'So . . .' said the museum guide, holding his torch under his chin so it gave his face a creepy glow and showed us way too much of what was up his nose. 'Who wants to hear about the Curse of the Cat of Kings?'

The hand of every kid in the room shot up, including mine and Pradeep's. This History Museum sleepover was turning out to be way cooler than I'd expected.

'Legend has it,' said the guide, 'that two grave robbers set off into the Egyptian desert to find the tomb of the Cat of Kings. Their goal: to steal the mummified cat's treasure! No one knows

exactly what happened, but days later the robbers were found wandering through the desert with layers of scarab beetles clinging to their backs!'

'Urrrgh!' I shuddered. I *really* hate bugs.

'The robbers had lost the ability to speak – so could tell no one what had befallen them.' He paused and looked around at our faces. 'They were the first victims of the Curse of the Cat of Kings. Thus the tomb remained undiscovered and intact . . . until earlier this year when builders unearthed it while digging the foundations for a new MoonBucks coffee shop.'

'The museum arranged for the whole tomb to be transported here,' Pradeep whispered. 'It's still sealed – so the museum scientists can excavate it and do loads of tests and stuff!'

'According to the legend, anyone not "pure of heart" who tries to enter the tomb will suffer the same fate as the Egyptian grave robbers,' the guide continued.

I blurted out, 'So the robbers couldn't make a single sound?'

'The robbers weren't mute,' the guide replied. 'Instead, the only sound they could make was *Miaoooooowwww!*'

The guide made a loud miaowing noise that suddenly turned into an 'Aaarrrraaagh!' His voice shot up to a squeal. He jumped up and the torch clattered to the floor. 'Something wet just bit me!'

Pradeep and I shot each other a look that said, 'FRANKIE?'

Frankie, my pet zombie goldfish, *really* doesn't like cats. Especially one particularly evil little kitten that belongs to my Evil Scientist big brother, Mark. I guess Frankie was thinking that

if a cat's miaowing at you, you bite it first and ask questions later! I glanced down at the mug of water that Frankie had been sitting in while we listened to the scary History Museum stories. Yep, he was definitely gone. This was bad for three reasons:

Firstly, even though he's a zombie, Frankie *is* also a goldfish, so he can't stay flopping around out of water for long.

Secondly, being a zombie goldfish, Frankie has the ability to zombify anyone that looks into his eyes, and we didn't want to end up with a lot of zombified kids in pyjamas mumbling, 'Swishy little fishy.'

Thirdly, when the museum guide squealed, all the kids jumped up from their sleeping bags and started to panic. So there were lots of feet stomping around on the same ground that Frankie was flopping about on.

'I can see Frankie!' Pradeep said. 'By the skirting board at twelve o'clock.'

I looked at him blankly.

Pradeep sighed. 'Twelve o'clock means straight ahead!' He pointed to the orange flash that was Frankie, who was slowly flopping towards us. 'I'll block – you take the mug and grab him!'

We threw ourselves into the mosh of screaming kids and sleeping bags, dodging flapping arms and stomping feet. Frankie made a dive over one particularly flappy kid's head, bounced off a Spider-Man pillowcase and landed with a splash back in the mug!

'You couldn't just sit and listen, could you, Frankie?' I whispered.

'My mum would say that you have a "low boredom threshold",' Pradeep added as he crawled over to join us. 'Come on – we've got to

find you better hiding place or we'll be thrown out of the museum and you'll be flushed down the loo.'

'The loo,' I said. 'That's it!'

'When in doubt,' we said at the same time, 'hide in the loos and figure it out!'

CHAPTER 2

NIGHT IN THE MUSEUM

Now, you might think hiding in the loos is a weird plan. But you would be amazed at how many times it has saved Pradeep and me.

1. When my Great-Aunt Celia (with the pointy prickly chin hairs) came round to visit – hiding in the loo meant successfully avoiding getting kissed.
2. When Miss Murdock was looking for volunteers to demonstrate country dancing in PE class, Pradeep and I hid in the loos for *so long* that Mrs Murdock thought we had bladder problems and

didn't make us dance for a *whole* term.

3. When Mark and Sanj (our Evil Scientist and Evil Computer Genius big brothers) invented a game called 'Moron Bowling', we hid in the loo at Pradeep's house for most of the day, until Sami, Pradeep's little sister, had to go and accidentally blow our cover.

'Stealth mode,' I whispered. Pradeep nodded. We each headed off in a different direction and slunk, snuck, edged, crawled and crept our way out of the activity room, through the main hall and towards the loos.

'We've got to get Frankie into something where he's safe, but he can't be seen,' Pradeep said, as soon as we had made it through the toilet doors. 'What have we got?'

Both of us emptied our pyjama pockets on to the floor. I had two pencils, a long piece of string from the inside sleeve of my jacket that I'd been pulling out bit by bit for months and only came loose this morning, a folded and paper-clipped fact sheet about ancient Egypt and my lucky-horseshoe-magnet key ring.

Pradeep had a pouch of kiwi juice left over from the museum packed lunch, a sheet of Egyptian stickers they gave us when we first got here, a laminated card from his mum with an alphabetical list of all his allergies and who to call in an emergency, and his super-waterproof submersible camping torch.

'The torch!' I said. 'It's perfect.'

Pradeep pulled out the batteries and bulb and stuff from inside. Then he filled it with water from the sink.

'What do you think, Frankie?' I asked, holding up his mug.

Frankie jumped straight into the water-filled torch and Pradeep screwed the clear plastic cover back on. Then we each filled our pyjama pockets again with our stuff.

'It sounds like it's quiet out there,' said Pradeep, listening at the toilet door. 'Now Frankie's safe, we should probably go back.'

We pushed the door open a crack and peered out. The shadow of the enormous diplodocus in the main hall filled the corridor. Light reflected off the swords of the knights at the entrance to the medieval exhibition and the flicker of the fake fire in the caveman's cave seemed to be saying, 'Why go back to the group and do worksheets . . . when you could explore?'

CHAPTER 3

THE MUMMY WALKS

'Let's take a look around!' I said to Pradeep.

'They won't do lights out for a while, I guess,' Pradeep mumbled.

Pradeep has an inbuilt fear of breaking rules, which he finds really hard to override. I find it kinda easy.

We slipped through the door. The rest of the kids were still in the sleepover activity room. Pradeep and I headed the other way towards the Egyptian exhibition. The torch sloshed slightly in my hands as Frankie swooshed about in there, pinging off the spring at the bottom as if he was in a fishy bouncy castle. Suddenly the end of the torch started to glow green.

'Wow, we've made a zombie goldfish torch,' Pradeep whispered.

'Cool,' I replied, but then I remembered something really important. 'Um, Pradeep, don't Frankie's eyes only glow like that when he senses some kind of trouble?'

As soon as the words left my mouth, I saw something move towards the giant doors of the Egyptian exhibition. It was the size of a small cat and had bandages trailing behind it. It skittered around a corner and disappeared.

I rubbed my eyes and looked again but it was gone.

'Did we just see the Cat of Kings?' My voice shook way more than I expected.

'Oh good,' Pradeep sighed.

'GOOD!' I whisper-yelled. 'How can that be *good*?'

'It's good that you saw it too,' Pradeep whispered. 'I thought I was seeing ghosts. Or undead mummies . . . or mummy ghosts.'

The green glow from our goldfish torch got brighter.

'Well, that's enough exploring for one night,' I said, trying to sound cool. 'I think I'm ready for some worksheets now. Maybe some colouring in . . .' I trailed off, hoping Pradeep would agree with me. But somehow Pradeep's 'Fear of Breaking Rules' dial had been turned all the way up to 'Be Brave at All Costs'.

'We have to follow it, Tom!' he whispered. 'This could be huge. What if it's the *actual* Cat of Kings? We could be the first people in the world to see it!'

There was no point arguing with Pradeep when he got like this. He was acting for the greater good of young archaeologists everywhere. He grabbed the torch and marched towards the huge stone doors that stood on either side of the Egyptian exhibition entrance. One had the face of a cat carved on the front and the other the face of a dog.

'They were really into their pet gods in Egypt,' I said as I stared at the giant animal faces and then down at Frankie. 'Do you think there was a god of goldfish?'

'Hatmehit,' Pradeep huffed.

'Bless you,' I said.

'No, the god Hatmehit,' Pradeep answered.

'Bless you again. It must be the dust in here . . .' I started to say.

'I'm not sneezing! That's the god's name – the god of goldfish.' Pradeep shook his head.

'No way! There's actually a god of goldfish?'

'Well, she's a goddess of protection that looks

like a fish, which is close enough,' Pradeep said, and shone the zombie fish torch at the faces on the entrance doors. 'I think this cat one is called Bastet and the jackal is Anubis.'

I stared hard at the jackal. 'It looks like a dog,' I said. 'How do you remember this stuff anyway?'

'I don't know,' said Pradeep. 'Egyptian stuff just stays in my brain. Come on. It must have gone this way.' Frankie waved his fin at me from inside the torch, motioning for me to follow.

I took one last look over my shoulder towards the sleepover activity room, then patted the cat god on its nose and followed Pradeep inside.

Immediately and silently, the doors swung shut behind me.

CHAPTER 4

A ROOM WITH A TOMB

'Ummm, Pradeep?' I muttered. I was going to explain that I thought I had just accidently shut us in the Egyptian exhibition with a potentially undead mummified cat and a *definitely* undead zombie goldfish by disrespecting some long-dead cat god. But then I thought better of it. Pradeep was so focused on looking for the Cat of Kings he hadn't noticed anyway.

Inside the Egyptian rooms, the walls were lined with huge stone tablets covered in hieroglyphic writing, and there were cabinets full of scrolls and jewellery. I pressed my face up against the glass. 'They liked to carve things into

bug shapes, didn't they?' I said with a shudder as I stared at all the beetle-shaped pins and stuff.

Pradeep was busy shining Frankie's torch all around the huge room. But there was no cat mummy in sight.

'Maybe we just saw a shadow?' Pradeep said, sounding disappointed.

The entrance to the tomb of the Cat of Kings stood before us. It was big. *Really big*. I mean, it was the grave of a cat, so I'd been thinking it would be pet-carrier sized.

'It's as big as a garage,' I said out loud. 'Why does one dead cat need all that space?'

'The Egyptians believed that you could take stuff with you to the afterlife. So they probably buried the cat with food, jewels, even servants,' Pradeep said.

'That's gotta be the worst job *ever*. Servant to a dead cat,' I muttered.

That's when we heard a crash. Frankie's eyes

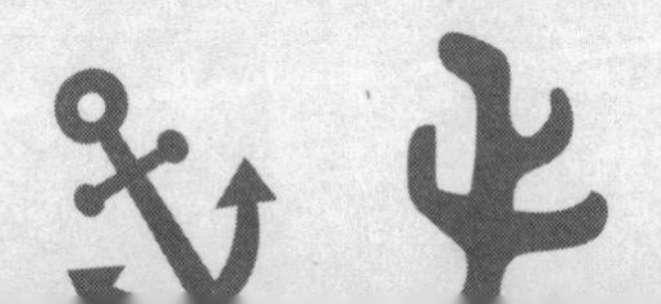

blazed so bright that the whole room was lit by a spooky green glow.

A flash of white moved behind one of the giant stone statues.

'The cat,' Pradeep whispered. He ducked underneath the red ropes that were there to protect the tomb and statues from museum visitors, and I followed. 'We have to be careful,' he said. 'We can't touch any of this stuff. It's very fragile.'

There was another crash.

'I don't think the Cat of Kings knows he's supposed to be careful,' I whispered.

'Come on,' Pradeep said, speeding up, 'before he gets away!'

We skidded to a halt next to a huge statue of a pharaoh. In the glow of green light we could see a bandage dragging along the ground behind the stand the statue was on. Then it disappeared.

'It's gone under the statue,' I cried. 'But that's impossible!'

'How did it do that?' Pradeep asked. He tapped at the base of the stand. 'Ah . . . it's hollow.'

'There must be a secret door or something,' I said.

Pradeep pushed and prodded at different bits of the stand. 'I think it must be a pressure pad,' he muttered.

Frankie had started to unscrew the top of the torch from the inside, so I opened it up and let him have a look. He leaped out and slammed himself against the stand, then plopped back into the torch with a splash. On his third slam, something gave way, and a hidden door flipped open like a giant cat flap.

'Frankie!' Pradeep and I yelled as he tumbled through the door and disappeared. I sprang forward and shoved my fingers in the gap, just as the flap swung closed.

'Oooooowwwww!' I yelled.

Suddenly Frankie's tail appeared out of the darkness. He must have been clinging to the lip of the flap with his teeth and had somehow managed to flip himself out through the tiny gap left by my fingers.

'The pencils!' cried Pradeep.

'This is no time for drawing!' I yelled. 'Get this flap off my fingers . . . it really hurts.'

'We can use the pencils you have in your pocket to prop open the flap!' he cried. He pulled them out of my pyjama pocket and wedged the flap wide open while I scooped up Frankie and put him back in the torch.

'Are you OK?' asked Pradeep.

'Yeah, I think so,' I said, looking at my bruised fingers. 'But don't you think we should go back now?'

'This is *history*, Tom,' said Pradeep. And with

that he threw himself feet first through the flap and down the metal chute.

'I think I preferred Pradeep when he was too scared to break the rules,' I whispered to Frankie, who just shook his head.

But I couldn't let Pradeep face the Cat of Kings alone. I took a deep breath, held on tight to the torch and threw myself head first after him.

CHAPTER 5

BENEATH THE MUMMY'S LAIR

I whooshed down a metal chute and landed on my face, right next to Pradeep. But before I could start yelling at him for jumping down secret passages without knowing what was at the bottom, I heard . . .

'Good evening, I've been expecting you,' followed by an evil wheeze.

'Sanj?' Pradeep and I said at the same time. We *really* need to stop doing that.

Frankie pressed his face against the front of the torch. His eyes were a wild green and his fins were clenched ready for a fight. He hates Pradeep's Evil Computer Genius big brother,

Sanj, *almost* as much as he hates my Evil Scientist big brother, Mark!

We seemed to be in some kind of ancient Egyptian evil lair. There were two big statues of Anubis behind us and pharaohs' heads and stuff leaning against the walls. Sanj's computer was in the middle of the room on top of a big old cabinet.

'Do you like it?' Sanj asked. 'It still needs a bit of work, but it's an evil home away from home.'

'How did you build this in the museum?' Pradeep asked.

'Technically we are behind the museum rather than *in* it,' Sanj said. 'This is the old site of the incinerator, which is underneath the alley at the back of the museum, and the chute from the Egyptian exhibition is where they used to put the rubbish.' He paused. 'Kind of fitting that you morons fell down a rubbish chute, don't you think?' He wheezed his pathetic evil laugh again.

Frankie was thrashing around so much inside the torch that it flipped right out of my hands and rolled underneath the cabinet.

'When Mark and I did our work experience here at half-term it was easy to gain access and turn it into the chic and modern lair you see today. There was loads of great stuff down here. Old exhibits . . . animatronics from the moving dinosaurs. It's all come in *very* useful.'

'So Mark is—' I started to say, when I was interrupted by a much more impressively evil, 'Mwahhaaa haaa haaa haaa haaa!'

'Here,' Pradeep finished for me.

'You losers were so easy to trick,' Mark said, stepping out of the shadows. He was holding a bubbling test tube of something green and toxic-looking. 'All I had to do was give Mum the flyer for this museum sleepover and you were both begging her to go.'

'Then we just had to lure you to our trap,' Sanj added.

A screeching 'Miaooooooww' came from the other side of the room.

'The cat mummy!' I cried. 'Sanj, Mark, look out!'

'Idiot,' Mark said, and scooped the cat up from the floor. He unwrapped what I could see now was a lot of toilet paper until it revealed his evil sidekick vampire kitten.

'Fang?' I mumbled.

Mark smiled. He scratched Fang behind her ears. 'Who's an evil mummy kitty then?' he cooed.

Suddenly Frankie launched himself out from under the cabinet in true ninja style.

'Frankie!' Pradeep yelled, as a flash of orange smashed Fang out of Mark's arms and on to the floor.

I shot Pradeep a look that said, 'He must have unscrewed the torch lid again while he was under the cabinet. Maybe he's trying to cause a distraction so we can escape.'

Frankie blindsided the kitten with his tail, but Fang flipped backwards and swiped at him with her needle-sharp claws. Frankie leaped up for another attempt at a face-slap, but Fang was too quick for him. She pinned him to the floor and licked her lips.

'Playtime's over, kitty!' Sanj shouted. 'You can't eat—'

'Zombify her, Frankie,' I interrupted. 'Do it now!'

Frankie stared hard at the kitten, his green eyes glowing brighter than ever, but Fang clamped her eyes shut lightning-fast and leaped away. As Mark scooped up his vampire kitten and put her in his Evil Scientist white-coat pocket, I hurried over and grabbed Frankie.

'When can I let her eat the fish?' Mark rolled his fingers into a fist.

'Soon,' Sanj said. 'But for now, we need the fish for our plan. Come on, keep up with the programme! And –' he turned to Pradeep – 'unbelievably, for this task we need *you* too.'

I rooted around under the cabinet and managed to find the torch and slip Frankie back inside. Sanj handed me a bottle of water to top it up before I screwed on the lid.

'We can't have the fish uncomfortable now, can we?' he said, smirking.

'Why would I help you?' Pradeep demanded.

'Because we're going to keep you trapped down here until you do,' Sanj replied, folding his arms and sitting down in an expensive-looking swivel chair next to the cabinet.

There was a whirring, crunching sound, and then the arms of the big Anubis statue behind Pradeep shot forward and trapped him in a bear hug.

CHAPTER 6

TRAPPED IN THE ARMS OF ANUBIS

'Arrggghh!' cried Pradeep.

'I've been dying to use that trap ever since we built it,' Sanj said, clapping his hands. 'That was part of an old moving dinosaur exhibit that we found down here. I think it's much better like this than wasted on some velociraptor, don't you think?'

I tried to pull the arms away from Pradeep, but Mark grabbed me and dragged me away. 'You and the fish gotta do whatever we want . . . or we might just forget to let your little friend outta here.' He grinned.

'OK,' I said, looking back at Pradeep. 'We'll

help you. What do you need us to do?'

Sanj pushed a button and a holographic 3D image appeared in front of his laptop, projected out into the room.

'Wow, good tech set-up for an ancient lair,' Pradeep said, and stopped wriggling.

'I know, I can't bear old things actually,' Sanj said, brushing the dust off his hands before he touched his computer keyboard again.

A map of the tomb above us appeared on the screen.

'How do you know what it looks like inside?' I asked.

'The museum archaeologists X-rayed it in preparation for the unsealing, which is scheduled for tomorrow.' Sanj smiled. 'That's why

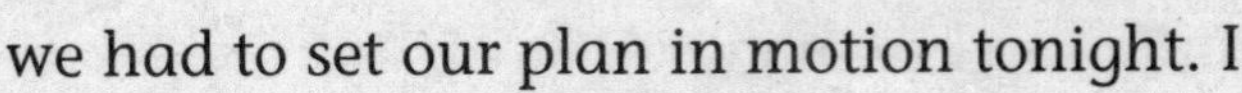

we had to set our plan in motion tonight. I

"borrowed" the map from the archaeologists' database. They really should improve their security.'

'All you have to do is take the fish, break into the tomb, bypass all the booby traps and open the sarcophagus to reveal the mummy,' Mark went on. 'Got it?'

'Um, booby traps?' I said.

'After that, you will *await* further instructions,' Sanj continued.

'How can I *await* instructions when I'm *in* the tomb?' I asked.

'Because your moron friend will be in your ear the whole time,' Mark said, shoving an earpiece into my ear. 'TESTING!' he yelled into the tiny microphone in his hand. I jumped back and rubbed my ear while he walked over and pinned the microphone to Pradeep's pyjamas.

Frankie was thrashing about so much in his torch that I had to hang on to it with both hands so I didn't drop him again.

'This is the prototype for my latest invention,' Sanj said proudly, holding up what looked suspiciously like a pair of ordinary glasses. 'I managed to sell the design to a computer company, which is how I managed to get enough money to kit out this lair. They are Anti-Hypno-Power Vision Super Glasses, or Hyp-Vis Specs as I prefer to call them. They're what all Evil Computer Geniuses and Evil Scientists will be wearing next year.'

Mark and Sanj put on their glasses and Sanj held a pair out for me.

'Why do I need to wear them? I don't think I'm the one who needs protection

against being hypnotized!' I looked down at Frankie, who nodded.

'If you wear them, then Pradeep will be able to see whatever you see and hear you when you speak,' Sanj replied. He slipped the Hyp-Vis Specs on to my face, and the image of what I was looking at came up on Sanj's laptop screen on the cabinet in front of Pradeep.

'Why do I need to see everything that Tom sees?' Pradeep asked.

'We need your mind, Pradeep, but frankly, Tom will be better at getting through the booby traps,' Sanj answered.

'And Frankie?' Pradeep and I said at the same time.

'Just get on with it!' Mark snapped. 'Take the fish and hurry up! There's a door over there that leads right into the museum.'

'Um, I knew that,' I said, and turned and headed for the door with the big 'Emergency Exit' sign over it.

Pradeep nodded to me. 'Good luck, Tom.'

Frankie's eyes were glowing bright as we climbed the stairs and walked towards the tomb of the Cat of Kings.

CHAPTER 7

RIDDLE ME THIS

'OK, Pradeep,' I said as I stared up at the tomb doors. 'See anything useful?' I turned my head to the left and right and up and down to give him a good look.

'Could you stop moving around so much, Tom?' Pradeep mumbled. 'You're making me feel sick.'

'Oh, sorry!' I said. I'd forgotten that Pradeep gets travel sick from pretty much every type of motion, except (weirdly) in boats.

'Wait! What's that?' Pradeep said. 'Over the door. There's writing in hieroglyphics.'

'It says, "Beware those who enter here with an

evil fart". . .' Pradeep and I both cracked up.

'I did not force you to do our evil bidding just so you could make Egyptian fart jokes!' Sanj shouted.

Then Pradeep interrupted. 'Wait. Oh, I see, sorry. It says, "Beware those who enter here with an evil heart". It says *heart*. Some hieroglyphic characters are about the meaning and some are about the sound. They're easy to mix up.'

Frankie's eyes dimmed from his 'high alert' bright green colour. I think he liked the fart joke too, which got me thinking – do goldfish fart? I asked Frankie.

'Stop it!' Sanj interrupted again. 'What does it say after that?'

I stepped closer to the message so Pradeep could read it.

'"Beware the Curse of the Cat of Kings" . . . blah, blah, blah . . . "the tomb is guarded by the emerald-eyed protector for whom the afterlife holds no fear",' Pradeep read. 'Ah, here we are. "Those who enter proud and true, the warm south sea will let them through".'

'I have no idea what that means,' I said, looking around.

'It's a riddle,' said Pradeep.

'Those who enter proud and true, the warm south sea will let them through,' I repeated.

'South!' Pradeep suddenly shouted. 'True south!'

'Not so loud,' I said, rubbing my ear.

'The entrance to the tomb is true south. We need a compass to work out which way that is.'

'Hang on, I can make one!' I cried. 'I saw it on a Grizzly Cook survival show.' I took the paperclip from the worksheet in my pyjama pocket and twisted a piece off it. Then I rubbed the magnet from my lucky-horseshoe key ring along the metal in one direction. I unscrewed the lid of Frankie's torch and asked him to swim to the bottom and stay still. Then I put the metal paper clip on the water.

'It's working!' I said proudly as the paperclip spun to a stop. 'One end should be pointing due north and the other due south. Even though I don't know which end is which, we've still got a one in two chance of getting it right.'

'Moron, did you just do something . . . smart?' Mark asked over the earpiece.

'Cool!' Pradeep said, sounding impressed.

I picked a direction and walked around to what looked like the back of the tomb. There was

a very thin stone door in the middle. 'Right, now we've got to get in,' I said.

'I think I've figured it out. It says, "Walk proud and true", so stand up tall, Tom,' Pradeep said.

Posture is not a big thing for me but I stretched up tall as I could.

'Then it says, "The warm south sea will let them through",' Pradeep went on.

With that, Frankie swam to the top of the torch, jumped out, landed on my head and spat water at the door. A low rumble echoed through the hall as the stone doors scraped aside.

'Wow,' breathed Pradeep. 'You did it! I wish I was there with you.'

Stale air hit me in the face. It smelt like thousand-year-old gym socks in there.

'You really don't, Pradeep,' I muttered, trying not to gag. 'You *really* don't.'

CHAPTER 8

A VERY PECULIAR PUZZLE

'You're in. Now hurry up and find that sarcophagus!' said Sanj's voice in my ear.

Frankie's eyes glowed brighter as we stepped into the cold of the tomb. Inside I saw three small doors: one on the left, one on the right and one straight ahead. Each door had one, two or three lines carved into it.

It was very dark, even though the main door remained open. I pulled my pyjama sleeves down and shivered. I would like to say it was just the cold, but I think it was more of a freaked-out shiver. I looked around the cramped hall for any hieroglyphic writing, but there was

nothing on the walls. Then I screwed the lid back on Frankie's torch and pointed him up at the ceiling.

'Hang on – there's something up here. I'll tilt my head right back so you can read it,' I said.

'"The first opens the second and the second opens the third. But the first will open to no one until the final note is heard",' translated Pradeep. 'I think the riddle relates to a musical scale!'

'That's easy!' I said. I closed my eyes and started to sing into the torch like it was a microphone. "Laaa, laaa, laaa, ooooh, baby, oooh!"

'STOOOOOOOOOOOOOPPPPPPPPPPPP!' Pradeep, Mark and Sanj screamed in my ear.

I opened my eyes. Rows of sharp wooden spikes were sticking out from the walls all around me.

'Your singing is *literally* lethal,' Sanj snapped. I could hear Fang in the background purring evilly.

'The room must be booby trapped!' Pradeep gasped. 'If you sing a wrong note, the spikes come out. The right notes must open the doors.'

I touched my finger to the wooden spike nearest me and it crumbled into dust. 'Phew,' I sighed. 'At least the spikes are too ancient to actually get me.'

'You are wasting our time,' Mark shouted down the microphone.

'OK, OK,' I said. 'I can whistle way better than I can sing. I'll try that.' Slowly and carefully, I started to whistle a scale. As I hit the first note

the door with two lines carved into it creaked open.

'It's working, Tom! Keep going,' Pradeep said.

As I whistled the second note, the door with three lines slid to one side. Only one door to go! I puckered my lips and whistled through the third, fourth and fifth notes. Nothing. I tried the sixth and seventh notes. Zip.

Finally I made my loudest whistle yet for the eighth and final note of the scale. Frankie was peeking out from behind his fins, so the room had gone very dark. Then I saw it – the final door, the one with just one line carved into it, was opening! I shone Frankie's torch towards the movement and . . . 'Buuuuuuuuuuuuuuuugs!' I shrieked in a voice so high that I'm pretty sure every dog within a two-mile radius heard me. It was not one of my proudest moments.

I threw myself back against the wall, turning most of the remaining spikes to dust, as thousands of beetles scuttled past my feet.

'What's going on?' Sanj shouted. 'Look down so we can see.'

I shook my head so fast it must have made Pradeep feel queasy. 'There are bugs. Hundreds of them! I *HATE* bugs!'

'Tom, try to look down at them,' Pradeep said calmly.

I tilted my head down and shone Frankie's torchlight at the moving floor, just as a breakaway team started crawling up my trainers.

'They're scarab beetles,' Pradeep said. 'They're not dangerous.'

I lifted my head to look at the doorway that the bugs were pouring from. There seemed to be a steep stone staircase just through the door.

'I think that's the door you have to go through, Tom,' Pradeep whispered.

'Why does it have to be the bug door?' I whimpered. 'There are two perfectly good bug-free doors I could go through.'

'Well,' said Pradeep, 'I know it's this door because there's a big arrow painted on the floor just inside the doorway with hieroglyphics that say, "Sarcophagus this way".'

I tried to force myself to step over the bugs, but it felt as if my feet were frozen to the spot.

'I can't get past them, Frankie,' I whispered. Frankie shook his head and shot me a look that was a combination of 'I can't believe you are this scared of a few bugs' and 'Don't worry, I'll take care of it'.

With a shaking hand I unscrewed the torch lid. Frankie poked out his head, nodded and then flung himself on to the bug-covered floor.

CHAPTER 9

STEP INTO THE MUMMY'S PARLOUR

Frankie swooshed and swished his way across the floor like a little orange bug duster, flicking beetles out of the way so I had a clear path to walk, although most of the scarab beetles had scuttled out through the tomb entrance anyway.

'Thanks, Frankie,' I whispered as he jumped back into the torch and I made my way to the staircase. 'Can you read these, Pradeep?' I asked, shining the torch at some hieroglyphics on the steps.

'It says,' Pradeep said, '"AND THEY'RE", on the first step, "CLIMBING" on the second, "A STAIRWAY", on the third and "TO HEAVEN", or

more accurately "THE AFTERLIFE", on the top step.'

'What? Like that really *long* song that Dad always plays in the car?' I asked.

'Maybe it's an old Egyptian song,' Pradeep replied.

As I neared the top step I whispered, 'Pradeep, you don't think the hieroglyphics mean that when you get to the top of this staircase, you face certain death or anything?'

'I think it's just leading you to the sarcophagus.' Pradeep answered. 'Don't worry.'

When I got to the room at the top, Frankie banged on the lid of the torch. I unscrewed the cover and he poked out his head, ready to take on whatever was waiting for us. The room was dark, with dead-looking once-flaming torches set in carved grooves in the walls and a stone bench in the centre.

'There's no sarcophagus!' Sanj shouted. 'It should be in this chamber!'

'Maybe an actual grave robber got here first,' I heard Mark say. Fang yowled in the background.

I walked to the centre of the room. I could just about stand up straight without my head touching the ceiling. Suddenly the torches on the walls burst into flames.

'That's weird,' Pradeep said. 'Those torches are thousands of years old. There must be some kind of sensor that registers when someone walks in. Whatever you do, *don't touch anything*, Tom. We don't know what might happen.'

'I promise I won't touch a thing,' I said. I sat down on the bench and crossed my arms. Then I got that funny feeling like when you're at the dentist's and the chair starts to move. I leaped up, but it was too late. The stone bench slowly sank down until it was completely flat in the floor. Then a scraping noise came from the stairway and a door rolled down from the ceiling, trapping me in the room.

'What was that?' Mark's voice yelled in my ear.

'Um, Pradeep . . .' I started to say, looking round the room in case anything else bad started happening. 'You know how I said I wouldn't touch anything. Well, that doesn't include sitting on stuff, *does it*?'

'What did you do, Tom?' he asked.

'Nothing!' I gulped.

Then, with a grinding noise, the ceiling started to move. The room was getting shorter, with me in it!

'Or maybe something . . .' I added. 'I think I've set off some sort of booby trap! The ceiling is coming down and I'm going to be flattened! What do I do?'

Frankie had jumped out of the torch and was standing on my head trying to push back the ceiling with his fins, but it wasn't making any difference.

'Look around!' cried Pradeep.

I looked up and down, not caring if I was making Pradeep sick with all the moving about. Frankie held on tight to my hair.

'Wait, I see something, just there,' Pradeep shouted. I stopped and looked at the tiny writing in the middle of the far wall.

'It says, "The path of the cat will lead through the door, follow the sun before the ceiling meets the floor".'

'I see a sun!' I cried, and half ran, half crawled over to the wall to look at it.

'Do the rays of the sun point at any thing?' asked Pradeep.

'Ummm, I don't know.' I was panicking now.

Frankie splashed back into the torch, then

popped his head out and pointed a fin at the longest rays of light painted around the sun. They were pointing down and to the right. 'Yes! This way,' I cried as I crawled over to the right side of the room as fast as I could.

Another sun was painted on this wall that seemed to be rising out of the stone floor like a sunrise. It made an arch on the wall just big enough for a cat to get through.

'It's a door!' Pradeep shouted down the mic.

'Or a cat flap,' I replied. 'I might be able to squeeze through. Mark's shoved me through the pet flap at our house so many times it's like I've been training for this my whole life! How do I open it?'

Then I spotted it. A goldfish-shaped groove cut into the stone of the door.

'Frankie!' I shouted. 'You're the key!'

Frankie took one look and threw himself out of the torch and into the fish-shaped hole. Immediately the door flipped back and I pushed

my way through, wriggling commando-style on the floor. Frankie jumped on to my back and hung on to my jacket as we slipped out of the room and into the darkness!

CHAPTER 10

FRANKIE AND THE SARCOPHAGUS OF DOOM

'What's going on?' Sanj screeched through the microphone. 'Have you reached the sarcophagus yet?'

My face hit the ground first. Again. I *have* to start going down slides the right way. I rubbed my head and opened my eyes but it was too dark to see anything. There wasn't even a green glow from Frankie's eyes.

'Frankie?' I called. There was a whoosh as torches on the walls burst into flame. The room I was in was about the same size as the one I had just escaped from but more colourfully decorated and with a higher ceiling. Two large statues – a

cat and a dog – stood at either end of the room and a large sarcophagus was in the centre. A stone table stood in front of the sarcophagus with a golden goblet on top.

'Yes!' I heard Sanj say. 'You're in the inner burial chamber. That's the sarcophagus of the Cat of Kings!'

Frankie jumped off my back and flopped into my hands. He'd been out of water for ages and needed to get back in, *fast*.

The torch! I'd managed to hold on to it as we squeezed through the cat flap, but all the water had spilt out as we slid down. What was I going to do? Suddenly Frankie leaped from my hand into the goblet on the little stone table.

'Frankie!' I started to shout, when I heard a splash of water. 'But how . . . ?' I said out loud.

'Never mind that,' Sanj interrupted. 'We have to get the coffin open.'

'And then you promise you'll release Pradeep?' I demanded.

'Sure,' Mark muttered.

I walked up to the sarcophagus and pushed at the lid. It didn't move. I heaved, I huffed, I strained, I shoved and I even *hove*. But it still didn't budge an inch. 'It won't move!' I yelled.

'Maybe there's some kind of riddle we have to solve to open it,' Pradeep said. 'Look around.'

'More riddles?' I sighed as I scanned the room.

There were a lot of little wooden and stone carvings of people lined up on the floor around the sarcophagus. They all seemed to have some kind of hieroglyphic painted on their chest.

'Those must be the servants for the cat in its afterlife,' Pradeep said. 'Can you line them up so I can see them?'

I lifted down the goblet with Frankie in it and he jumped out to help me. While Frankie was pushing figurines around, I ran my hands over the sarcophagus lid. There were four grooves, one carved into each corner, each about the same size and shape as one of the figures.

'Pradeep, there are four spaces on the coffin lid where the little carved servants would fit perfectly. Maybe we're supposed to spell something out to open the lid?'

'But what?' Pradeep said, thinking aloud.

'Maybe it's just his name?' I replied. 'King Cat. Or Cat King. Or Kingy, Kingy Kitty-Cat?'

'It must be the word "cat"!' Pradeep interrupted.

'"Cat" doesn't have enough letters,' I said. 'Even *I* know that!'

'In Egyptian it does. It has three hieroglyphics that make a sound and one that tells you what it is.'

Pradeep directed me and I set the carved figures up. Then I grabbed Frankie's goblet and stepped back.

Nothing happened.

'Try saying it out loud,' Pradeep said.

'How am I supposed to know how to say "cat" in Ancient Egyptian?' I spluttered.

'MiaaoOOOw!' screeched Fang in the background.

'Fang's right!' Pradeep said. 'It sounds like "Miaow!"'

Frankie looked at me as if I was betraying all of fish-kind by even thinking about making a cat noise.

'Sorry, Frankie, but I have to do this,' I said. And then I let off a very loud, 'MIIAAOOOOOWWWW!'

Very slowly, the lid of the sarcophagus started to creak to one side to reveal the mummy of the Cat of Kings. It was much, *much* smaller than I thought it would be. In fact, it was tiny!

'All this, just for you?' I whispered.

As the lid finally stopped moving, I heard a truly evil 'Miiaaaoooow', and suddenly Mark ran into the chamber carrying Fang.

CHAPTER 11

PROTECTOR OF THE CAT OF KINGS

'How did you get here so fast?' I asked, jamming a hand over the top of Frankie's goblet so he couldn't leap out and start a fight.

'All the booby traps have been disabled and the front door of the tomb has opened, so I could walk right in.' Mark grinned, readjusting his earpiece.

'Pradeep,' I called out, 'can you still see everything? Did they free you like they promised?'

'Pradeep isn't trapped by the stone statue any more, so we've kept our word,' Sanj replied.

'Technically,' Pradeep said. 'Now I'm tied

up over by the cabinet instead. It's a bit more comfortable, but I'm not free.'

'This is not the time for chit-chat,' Sanj interrupted. 'We need to move on to the next stage of our evil plan!'

'Aren't you scared of the curse?' interrupted Pradeep. 'Mark and Fang are hardly "pure of heart".'

'I don't believe in any stupid curse!' spluttered Sanj. 'You've annoyed me now, so I'm going to put you back in the grip of the Anubis statue!'

Mark grinned at me. 'Now the dead cat is ours we're going to—'

'Try not to let the cat out of the bag, Mark!' Sanj interrupted.

'Miiiaaoooow w,' screeched Fang.

'Not a literal cat in a literal bag,' Sanj sighed over the earpiece. 'Really, people. We need to find one last thing before we can . . . continue with our evil plan. We need the heart of Bastet.'

'And how are you going to get that?' I asked. Frankie was nipping my fingers now, trying to escape, but I made sure I held on tight.

'We aren't,' Sanj replied. '*You* are. I have to monitor things from the Egyptian evil lair to make sure everything goes to plan.'

'The cat statue over there is the one we need,' Mark said, pointing at the big statue at one side of the room. 'The heart is some kind of stone. You need to get it out, and I'm here to make sure you do it right!'

Fang hissed from Mark's pocket.

'You're gonna help us too, Fish!' Mark leaned towards the golden cup. 'Or Pradeep gets a big

cuddle from the stone statue!'

Sanj spoke up. 'Pradeep is back in the statue's grip, so you *have* to do want we want, both of you!'

'Fine,' I muttered. 'But after this, you have to let us both go!'

'Yes, yes,' agreed Sanj.

Carefully I lifted my hand off the top of the goblet. Frankie's fins were clenched ready for a fight, but he allowed himself to be poured back inside the torch without attacking Fang.

I looked up at the two big statues as I screwed on the torch lid.

'Are you OK, Pradeep?' I asked.

'I'm OK,' Pradeep replied. 'Let's finish this.'

CHAPTER 12

NOT A STONE TO BE SNEEZED AT

'According to Sanj's research, the heart of Bastet should be about the size of a ping-pong ball and is hidden inside the cat statue,' Pradeep said.

I looked at the statue of the cat god. In its hand was a tablet covered in hieroglyphics. I looked at it closely so Pradeep could see.

'It says, "Follow the scent to the heads of the gods. Pick both stones together to increase your odds",' Pradeep translated.

'This is lame. Why can't they just give us a map?' Mark grumbled.

'So we need to climb up to the statues' heads? I asked.

'I think so,' said Pradeep. 'And it sounds like you need to get something from both statues at the same time.'

'I'll do the cat one, you do the dog,' Mark snapped. 'Man, I'm gonna scuff my trainers climbing this.'

It didn't take long to scramble up the statues. I propped Frankie's torch on top of the dog's head. 'What now?' I called.

'I suppose you need to get to the heart of the statues somehow,' Pradeep answered.

I looked at the dog's nose. 'There's an opening in one nostril,' I told Pradeep. 'Do you think we have to reach inside the statues to get the stones out?'

'YES!' Pradeep replied. 'That's

what the clue means. You and Mark will have to "pick both stones together to increase your odds"! Like picking a nose!'

'I've gotta pick the nose of a giant stone cat-god statue?' Mark moaned. 'Gross.'

'I can't get my hand in – the hole's too small,' I called. 'We might have to use Frankie and Fang instead.'

'Whoever gets the stones, just remember you have to do it at the same time,' Pradeep added.

I unscrewed the lid of Frankie's torch so he was ready to jump. Mark and I looked at each other. 'One . . .' I said. 'Two . . .' Then Fang leaped out of Mark's pocket, scrambled on to the nose of the cat statue and thrust her paws deep into its right nostril. 'You were supposed to wait for three!' I shouted.

'Cats can't count,' Mark shouted as the statues started to shake. 'Just get the fish in there now!'

'What's happening?' Pradeep asked.

'I think the statues are mad at us for not

picking their noses at the same time!' I replied as Frankie leaped into the dog's left nostril.

I shoved my fingers in after Frankie. The hole was thick with dust and some kind of slime. I could just feel the edge of something round and cold with the tips of my fingers, but I couldn't get a grip on it!

Mark was shouting, 'Come on, kitty, you can do it!'

Then I felt Frankie push something cold and round towards my hand. A few seconds later I pulled out a round blue stone with Frankie stuck to the back of it. I dropped him back into the torch.

'Good Fang!' cooed Mark as his evil kitten fished out a ball of the same size but a snowy marbled pink colour from the cat god's nose.

'The quartz heart of Bastet!' Sanj clapped.

The statues were shaking so hard now that they had started to tilt forward alarmingly.

'They're going to fall!' I shouted.

I shoved the stone into my pyjama pocket and quickly screwed up Frankie's torch. Then I held on to the dog's neck for dear life.

'Hold tight, Mark!' I shouted.

'Miiiaaooooow!' Fang screeched.

A second later there was a small bump as stone met stone. I opened my eyes to see that the two statues had fallen nose to nose and were propping each other up.

'Phew,' I sighed as Mark and I climbed down. Fang's evil miaowing had turned into a purr.

'She knows it's nearly dinner time,' Mark whispered, grabbing the torch.

'Hey!' I cried, trying to grab it back, but Mark held the torch up out of my reach and shoved me away.

Then he took some electrical tape out of his Evil Scientist coat pocket and wrapped it around the lid to make sure it stayed on.

'Don't want him getting out too soon!' Mark laughed his loudest Evil Scientist laugh. 'And don't try and grab the fish again or I'll get Sanj to give his little brother a hug!'

'Are you quite finished?' Sanj snapped over the earpiece. 'We need to get the stone in place. The transformation has to happen tonight.'

'Transformation?' I asked.

'That's what I'm calling it,' Sanj replied. 'Put us on video on your phone, Mark. Now we have everything we need it's too late for them

to stop our evil plan anyway. Can you see me? Right.' He took a deep breath. 'We call it the "transformation", because it's a bit long-winded to say the "reanimation of the powerful Cat of Kings mummy using the combination of an ancient sacred stone and the zombification stare of an undead zombie goldfish".'

'What?' I said.

'We'll use your fish and this stone to create a reanimated zombie cat mummy slave, which we'll use to take over the world!' Mark snapped.

'Oh no!' Pradeep and I gasped at the same time.

'Send the kitten back to pick up the mixture. It looks like it's ready,' Sanj ordered.

Mark patted Fang on the head and she slunk out of the door of the tomb.

CHAPTER 13

THE MUMMY RETURNS

While Mark was looking at the weird pink stone and fiddling around with some ropes he'd brought with him, I crept over to his phone, which was propped up on the lid of the sarcophagus. I gave Pradeep a look that said, 'We can't let them do this. We need a plan.'

Then I said out loud, 'Does that writing say anything helpful?'

I'd noticed more hieroglyphics inside the coffin, including a picture of a weird fish with glowing eyes.

‘It says, “Grave robbers beware. The Cat of Kings is watched by the emerald-eyed protector for whom the afterlife holds no fear”.’

‘Didn’t it say that before? When we were first trying to get in?’ I asked. ‘But what’s that got to do with that little drawing of a fish?’

‘I have no idea,’ Pradeep replied. ‘The Egyptians had a lot of animal gods. Maybe they protected each other on some kind of rota?’

Then he shot me a look that said, ‘There’s more to say but I’ve lost my juice and stickers and am very unhappy to be stuck in the Anubis statue right now so can’t really talk.’

I gave him a look that said, ‘Sorry, Pradeep! You’re so upset that your looks aren’t really making sense. We’ll stop them. I’m just not sure how right now.’

Then I put my hand on the screen and said out loud, ‘I’m sorry you’re stuck being Sanj’s prisoner while I have to do all the dangerous archaeology stuff out here.’

Pradeep just rolled his eyes and shook his head.

Mark placed the heart of Bastet into a dip on a stone ledge that jutted out from the lid of the coffin. It fitted perfectly. Even though the pink quartz was hazy, you could still just about see through it.

'Stage two complete,' said Sanj. 'Now it's perfectly placed to illuminate the head of the mummy.'

I looked over at Mark, holding Frankie in the torch. 'You're going to shine Frankie's zombie stare through the heart of Bastet, aren't you?' I asked.

'Position the fish,' Sanj commanded.

Mark took the torch over to the sarcophagus lid. At that moment Fang bounded back into the tomb with a test tube of green liquid clenched in her teeth.

Mark reached down and took it. 'Good kitty,' he cooed.

Fang hissed.

'I mean bad kitty. Very evil, bad kitty.' Fang purred and rubbed against his leg.

Mark hooked the test tube up to a rope he'd suspended above the head of the cat mummy and took out the stopper.

'The toxic zombie goo will drip on to the mummy while Frankie's zombie stare shines through the heart of Bastet,' Sanj explained. 'If all goes to plan, the cat will be reanimated as a super-zombie mummy cat slave, and it will be entirely under *my* control.'

'*Our* control!' growled Mark.

'Quite,' said Sanj.

Mark positioned the golden goblet on the stone table behind the heart of Bastet and started to untape the torch lid so he could pour Frankie in. As soon as Mark took off the cover, Frankie leaped up and fin-slapped him across the face.

'You'll regret that, Fish!' yelled Mark.

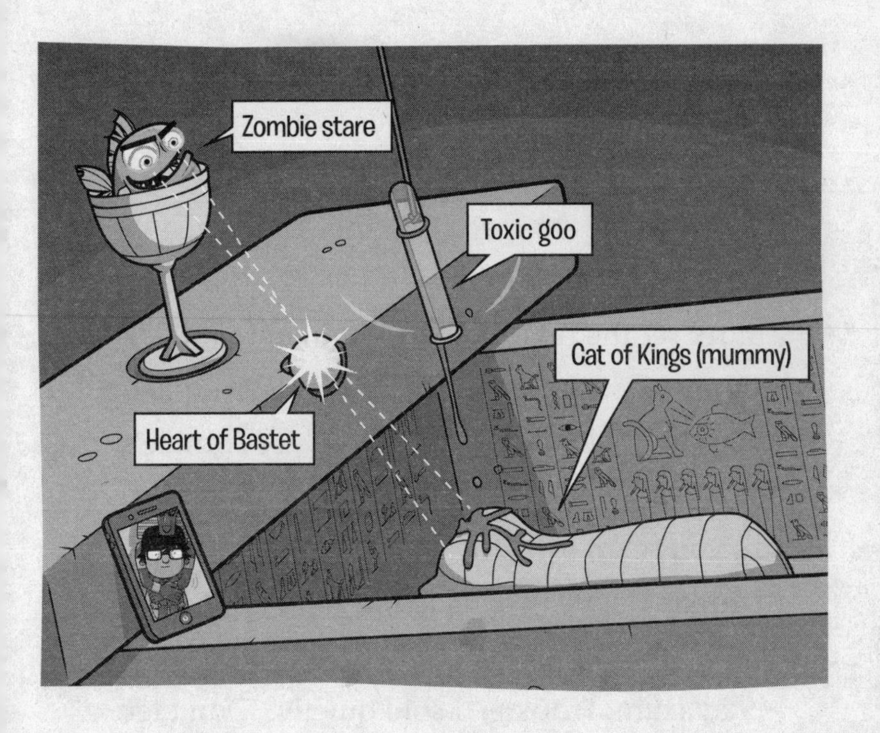

Suddenly we heard Pradeep shout, 'Ouch! Ouch! ARGHHH!' It sounded as if the arms of the Anubis statue were tightening around him.

'Stop it, Sanj!' I shouted.

Mark's phone screen showed Pradeep wriggling in the grip of the statue.

'The fish can stop me pressing this button at any time,' Sanj answered.

Frankie stopped fin-slapping Mark and plopped into the goblet.

'Perfect!' Sanj laughed.

Pradeep had stopped shouting. The statue must have released its grip.

Mark set the toxic goo dripping on to the mummy by swinging the vial over its head like a pendulum. Then he flicked the side of Frankie's goblet to get his attention. 'Hey, Fish, not long until you're an evil kitty snack!'

Frankie popped his head out of the water and his eyes went bright green.

'Stay calm, Frankie,' I said quietly. 'Don't let them make you mad.'

'Fancy some zombie sushi, Fang?' Mark said, leaning over the sarcophagus so his head was right next to the Cat of Kings.

That was all it took! Frankie's zombie stare shot from his eyes, aiming straight for Mark. But the quartz heart of Bastet was in the way. Frankie's stare went straight through the heart and out the other side in a rainbow of colours.

That had never happened before!

'Frankie, stop!' I yelled. But it was as if he was in some kind of trance.

The sarcophagus rattled and shook as Mark stood up and adjusted his Hyp-Vis Specs.

'Why is it taking so long?' Sanj snapped.

Then Mark looked at the toxic goo that was dripping on the mummy. He held out his finger and caught a drop, sniffed it, then licked it.

'Kiwi?' he yelled.

CHAPTER 14

THE GREAT ESCAPE

'Somebody ruined my toxic goo!' Mark shouted, grabbing me by my pyjama top and balling his fist.

On the phone screen, I saw Pradeep slip out from the grasp of the statue and walk towards the camera.

'That would be me,' he said, picking up a handful of spare computer cables.

'What?' said Sanj and Mark at the same time.

Mark uncurled his fist, but he didn't let go while Fang gave me evil looks from his pocket.

There was a scuffling sound and then Pradeep turned the laptop round so the camera showed both himself and Sanj, who was wrapped up in his Evil Computer Genius swivel chair with computer cables like a fly wrapped up by a spider.

'Curse this Evil Computer Genius swivel chair!' yelled Sanj. 'How did you ruin the gunge? You were my prisoner the whole time!'

'Not the *whole* time.' Pradeep smiled. 'You briefly released me from the Anubis statue and tied me up near the laptop. All that time I had been holding on to my laminated allergy list. I'd sharpened and serrated one of the edges, just in case I ever needed it to cut myself free from anything. Think about it, Sanj. That's why I never complain about carrying it around!'

'Of course!' grumbled Sanj.

'Once I was free and you were distracted by what was going on with Tom and Mark, I swapped the contents of my kiwi-juice pouch from my museum packed lunch for the toxic goo. Then I sat back down and made it look like I'd been tied up all along.'

'You could have been a good evil sidekick after all – if *only* you had been evil,' Sanj admitted.

'But that's not all . . .' Pradeep went on.

'It's not?' I interrupted, trying and failing to get away from Mark and Fang. 'Not that it's not really interesting and everything, but Frankie is still doing his zombie stare at the cat mummy, and even if it's not bringing it back to life, it's definitely doing something!'

'But don't you want to know how I got out of the death grip of the Anubis?' Pradeep asked.

'I do,' Sanj said.

'Yeah, I kinda do too,' admitted Mark.

'Miaow,' Fang agreed.

'The first time that you trapped me with the statue, I realized that it was controlled by sensor points on the arms that received a light signal from your laptop,' Pradeep said proudly.

'Well, that's pretty obvious,' Sanj huffed.

'So when you tried to imprison me the second time I was ready with my Egyptian stickers to cover the sensors. Then I just pretended that the arms were tightening around me whenever you pressed the button on the computer.'

'So you were just acting being trapped and in pain?' I said. 'You were really good.'

'Thanks,' said Pradeep. 'I tried to give you a look to tell you what was going on, one that said, "There's more to the plan! I've used my juice and stickers and am pretending to be unhappy to be stuck in the Anubis statue right now, so I can't really talk." But you didn't understand.'

'Ahhhhh, that makes sense.' I nodded. 'Sorry I doubted you!'

'And now I'm coming to help you,' Pradeep

shouted, and disappeared from the picture.

'No, come back here! That's not fair!' Sanj called after him, frantically unwinding himself from the cables.

At that moment, the sarcophagus started to shake so violently that Mark's phone fell to the floor. Mark finally let go of me and lunged for his mobile.

'The moron fish is doing something that's really not good, and the kiwi juice didn't do anything – so I'm thinking we just leave the fish here and leg it,' Mark yelled.

'No!' screamed Sanj over the earpiece. 'You have to stay there. I'm on my way!'

'No way am I being stuck in a tomb with some old dead cat,' Mark objected, and Fang miaowed in agreement. He grabbed my arm and started marching me towards the main door to the tomb.

'Frankie!' I yelled, pulling in the other direction.

Suddenly Sanj appeared in the doorway and Mark let me go in surprise.

How had he got here before Pradeep? I shook my head in confusion.

'I've brought more of the toxic goo you made earlier. We have to try again,' Sanj said.

'Fine,' grumbled Mark, looking longingly at the exit.

As they walked towards the shaking sarcophagus I jumped behind the fallen statues. I had to stop them and save Frankie, but how?

Just then, Pradeep stepped out of the shadows of the doorway. 'We've got to stop Sanj,' he said in his look. 'I think he's got a Plan B if Plan A

doesn't work, and I think Plan B is even worse!'
He stepped back into the darkness.

The sound of stone sliding across stone filled the room. The sarcophagus had stopped shaking and the lid was closing!

'Frankie!' I shouted, and sprang out of my hiding place.

CHAPTER 15

MAKE YOUR OWN MUMMY

Frankie was flapping around on the floor next to the sarcophagus. He must have flipped right out of the goblet when his weird zombie stare trance was broken by the closing lid.

'He needs water!' I cried as Mark grabbed me and pinned my arms to my sides. 'Let me go!'

'As long as the fish is alive there will be just enough power left in him for one more task,' Sanj replied. 'Then you can let Fang have her fishy snack,' he added to Mark.

Fang jumped out of Mark's pocket and slunk towards Frankie, licking her lips. That's when Sanj pounced. He scooped up Fang

and wound her tight in a bandage.

'Hey!' Mark let go of me and stepped forward. 'No one touches my evil kitten!'

At the same time, Sanj pulled some kind of weird ray gun with a big funnel on the front out of his pocket and pointed it at Mark.

'Don't make me use this,' he warned.

'Is that another hypno-ray? I'm wearing your Hyp-Vis Specs, remember? It won't work on me.' Mark balled his fist.

Sanj shrugged and pulled the trigger. A long string of white stuff shot out from the funnel and snaked around Mark until his whole body was tightly wrapped in bandages.

'It's my new mummy gun. Thought it might come in handy if we decided to make more mummies later on.' Sanj smiled. 'Always good to give these things a test run!'

Mark teetered like one of his own Moron Bowling pins and fell over. Then Sanj turned the gun on me.

'Don't move, or you'll be next!' he threatened. I looked desperately at Frankie, who had stopped flapping around by now, but I didn't dare move a muscle.

Pradeep would have a plan, I just knew it!

'Now I have your evil little kitten I can make her into my zombie mummy slave instead,' Sanj said to Mark. 'She'll still be a powerful zombie

slave, even if she isn't an ancient mummy.'

'Fang! No!' Mark pleaded.

Pradeep peered around the doorway at me. His look said, 'I know we really don't get on with Fang and she's definitely evil – but we can't let Sanj make her into a zombie cat mummy.'

'Agreed,' my look replied. 'And we have to save Frankie!'

Fang was struggling to free herself from the bandages but they held tight. Sanj positioned her on the sarcophagus lid and then lifted Frankie back into his goblet. As soon as Frankie hit the water his gills flapped slightly.

'Phew!' I sighed. I gave Pradeep a look that said, 'Frankie's OK!'

Sanj tapped on Frankie's goblet. 'Looky, looky, little fishy! Is that an evil kitty on the coffin lid over there? You'd better zombify her before she attacks!'

Frankie looked dazed and exhausted, but when he locked eyes on Fang on the other side

of the heart of Bastet, his eyes practically bulged out of his head.

'No, Frankie!' I yelled. 'Don't do your zombie stare!'

'Now, Tom!' Pradeep shouted at the same time. He leaped out of the shadows and tackled Sanj around the ankles. It was a tackle that any rugby coach would have been proud of, even though *technically* it was caused by Pradeep tripping over his shoelaces. Still, he managed to distract Sanj and knock him off balance!

At the same time, I grabbed Fang, but as I did I knocked the ping-pong-ball-sized heart of Bastet, which started rolling across the lid of the sarcophagus.

'Fang!' Mark shouted.

'I've got her!' I yelled back. 'OUCH!' She clamped her teeth into my hand.

Meanwhile, Frankie leaped out of the goblet and stopped the stone just before it rolled off the lid.

Sanj finally broke free of Pradeep's ankle grip and lunged for the stone, grabbing it from Frankie and holding it up high.

'You ruined my plan yet again!' Sanj yelled, pointing his weird gun at Pradeep and me in turn. 'But at least I still have the stone. As long as I have the heart of Bastet then I can still create a zombie mummy slave. I'll make a new mummy soon and then you won't be able to stop me!'

He did his eerie evil wheeze.

CHAPTER 16

RAIDERS OF THE LOST TOMB

I looked at Frankie. He knew exactly what to do. In a single spinning kung-fu move, he leaped into the air and slammed all his force into a single tail thwack aimed at the heart of Bastet. He splashed back into his goblet as the pale pink stone hurtled towards the floor.

'Nooooo!' Sanj screamed. The heavy stone slammed on to the toes of his right foot and then bounced off and shattered on the floor. 'Nooooo!' he yelled again, kicking the sarcophagus with his left foot in fury. Then he screamed again and clutched his toes. This time with no recognizable words.

By now, Fang had managed to slice through all her bandages (and some of my pyjamas) so I let her go. She ran over to Mark and licked his face. Then she ran her razor-sharp claws down the bandages trapping him, cutting him free.

'OUCH!' Mark winced. 'That was a little too close!' Then he added, 'Hey, what's that rumbling sound?'

'Pradeep,' I panted, 'does that sound to you like a big stone door slowly rolling closed?'

We looked towards the main doorway.

'It *is* a big stone door slowly rolling closed,' he confirmed. 'We've gotta get out of here!'

'Come on,' I shouted to Mark. 'Let's go!'

'That's what I said earlier . . . but no one listens to the Evil Scientist big brother, do they?' Mark muttered as he scooped up Fang and put her in his pocket.

Sanj was hobbling on his sore feet.

'Come on!' Pradeep yelled, pulling him along. 'We need to go, *now*.'

I grabbed Frankie's goblet and ran.

The rumble of the stone door sliding towards the floor pounded in our ears. It was halfway down already. We had to duck to get through!

'We're safe!' I sighed as we finally all made it outside.

Then, behind us from the tomb I heard a 'Miaoooooowwww!' and a splat. I looked down at the water-filled but fish-free goblet in my hand. 'Frankie?' I said.

'Where's Fang?' said Mark looking in the pockets of his Evil Scientist white coat.

Then we all looked towards the *almost* closed door.

'Kitty, come here!' cried Mark, shoving his hands into the rapidly shrinking gap between the door and the floor.

'How can we distract Fang?' Pradeep asked. 'If we can get her to leave Frankie alone for a second, maybe we can grab them both?'

'I've got an idea!' I cried. It was as if a light

bulb had been turned on inside my head. 'What can't any cat resist?' I started digging in my pyjama pocket.

'Of course!' said Pradeep. 'It's kryptonite for cats!'

'String!' we cried together.

I shoved the end of the string through the gap and wiggled it. In a second I felt the snatch of claws. I yanked hard and managed to drag Fang

through the tiny gap with the string between her paws and an orange tail hanging out of her mouth. She spat Frankie on to the floor and grabbed playfully at the end of the string again with wide-eyed wonder – as if she had never seen such an amazing thing as string before in her little evil life!

Frankie spat water at her and then jumped back into the goblet, just as the door closed so firmly that a piece of paper could barely fit underneath.

CHAPTER 17

A MUMMY'S JOB IS NEVER DONE

Mark scooped up Fang and put her in his pocket just as torchlight hit our faces.

'What are you kids doing back here?' cried a voice. It was one of the museum guides. I shoved the goblet behind my back.

'The doors to the Egyptian rooms were stuck fast. It took us ages to get them open,' another voice said. 'And there were some very funny noises.' He looked around suspiciously.

'We were just about to call lights out for the sleepover when we did a head count and saw you were missing,' said the first guide. 'Or at least, two of you were.' He turned to the other

guide and muttered, 'We must have done the count wrong. There are four of them here, not two.'

'My brother hurt his feet when he was climbing over those red ropes that you're not supposed to cross,' Pradeep said with a smile at Sanj.

'We were looking for someone to help him,' I added.

The museum guides helped Sanj up. 'We'll make sure you're OK, son,' said the first one, 'but you shouldn't ever go behind the ropes like that. We'll have to call your parents about this and ask them to come and collect you.'

'Let's get you to the first-aider,' the other said.

A happy miaow came from Mark's pocket.

'What's that?' the first guide said, looking at Mark. 'You brought a cat . . . into a museum? That's it. We're calling your parents too!'

'You can't call miaow . . . miaow . . . m . . . m . . . my . . . *miaow*!' Mark said and grabbed his mouth with his hands. Fang peered up out of his pocket and purred.

'No good being smart with us, son,' the guide snapped. 'We'll find out who your parents are and call them anyway.'

I shot Pradeep a look that said, 'Is Mark really miaowing?'

Sanj looked over at Mark and shook his head. 'Listen,' he started, 'you've got this all wrong. There's really no need to call miaow . . . my . . . miaow parents, miaow, miaow, *miaow*!' Sanj's eyes widened as he realized miaows were coming out of his own mouth too.

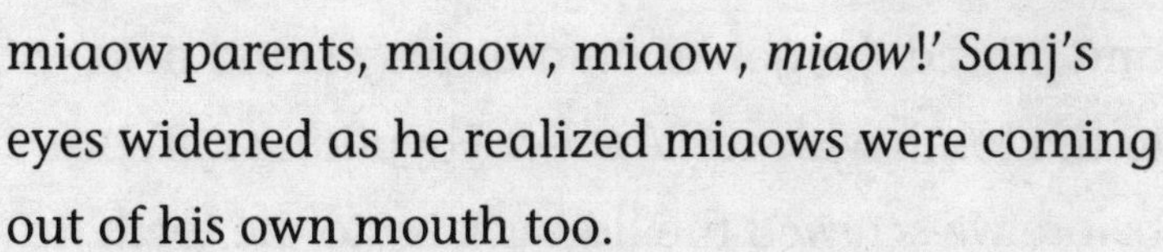

'You too, huh? You think this is funny?' the second guide snapped.

'Miaow, miaow, *MIAAOOOWWW*!' Sanj shouted, turning red with rage.

'It's the Curse of the Cat of Kings!' Pradeep whispered. Out loud he said, 'Our mum's phone number is on this emergency card,' and handed the guide his laminated allergy list.

'Thanks,' the guide said as they led Mark and Sanj away. 'You boys head back to the group now, lights out in two minutes.'

'OK,' we promised. We could hear them miaowing all the way down the corridor.

'I guess they weren't "pure of heart" when they entered the tomb,' I said.

'The curse must kick in when you leave,' Pradeep replied. 'I wonder if it will wear off?'

We poured Frankie back into Pradeep's torch and placed the goblet on a display stand next to the tomb with some other Egyptian stuff. Just before we screwed the lid back on to the torch, a funny-looking sheet of paper slid out from under the door of the tomb.

'Do you think there's someone still in there?' I asked. 'We should call the guides!'

'No – wait.' Pradeep was turning the paper around in his hands. 'It's papyrus.'

'What does it say?' I asked.

'It's written in "hieratic", which is like handwritten hieroglyphics. I don't know if I'm reading it right, but I *think* it says, "Dear emerald-eyed protector and your brave boy slaves . . ."'

'Boy slaves!' I repeated. I could swear Frankie was smiling.

'"As per the prophecy, you have protected my tomb from those with evil in their hearts. Now the heart of Bastet is beyond use and I can finally truly rest. Cats do need a lot of sleep. K of C."'

Pradeep and I looked down at Frankie who shrugged and winked at us.

'There's more,' Pradeep said. 'It says, "PS If you still have the heart of Anubis . . ."'

I looked in my pyjama jacket pocket and pulled out the heavy blue stone.

'". . . the curse will be lifted if those affected lick the stone. PPS It tastes horrible."'

I smiled at Pradeep. 'Maybe we won't tell Mark and Sanj about the cure just yet?'

Pradeep smiled and turned to Frankie. 'Good work, Frankie. Just don't expect us to really be your "boy slaves" from now on.'

Frankie gave us a disappointed look.

'Maybe just this once,' Pradeep and I agreed.

When we got back to the group we all had a torchlight midnight feast of gummy scarab beetles and kiwi juice. We had positioned our sleeping bags behind a pillar so the guides couldn't see us. Pradeep took the piece of papyrus and fanned Frankie while I fed him bits of green candy.

'Do you think you would have liked living in ancient Egyptian times, Tom?' Pradeep asked.

I looked at the green candy beetle in my

hand. 'No way! Too many bugs,' I replied with a shudder. 'But I'm sure Frankie would have *loved* it.'

SPORTS-DAY SHOWDOWN

CHAPTER 1

ON THE ROAD AGAIN

The school track team took up the whole back row of the bus. They were playing 'Laugh or Loser!', a game that involved pulling faces at drivers behind us. If the drivers laughed, they got the thumbs-up. If they got angry, the whole track team made 'L for Loser' signs and stuck their tongues out.

'I don't really get the point of that game,' Pradeep groaned, lining up a full sick bag on the floor with several others. 'New bag!'

'I think the point of the game is that it has no point,' I replied. 'I mean, if you got more points for getting a little old lady to shout at you than

a lorry driver, then that might be more of a challenge . . .' I noticed Pradeep's green colour getting worse. 'Sorry!' I quickly handed him the first bag that came to hand. As he opened the top, a flash of orange burst out.

'Mmmmmm?' Pradeep squealed as Frankie, my pet zombie goldfish, clamped his mouth shut with his fins.

'Whoops! That must have been the one I put Frankie in,' I muttered. I handed Pradeep a fresh bag as Frankie plopped back into his water-filled one. 'I guess he wanted to make sure that you weren't going to heave on him,' I added, placing Frankie on my lap while Pradeep was sick. Again.

We were on our way to the Countywide Inter-Schools Intellectual Sports Day Challenge. On our coach were the netball team, the track team and the football team – who were going to take part in the sporty events. Plus the chess team, the poetry society, and the knitting, cooking and quilting clubs – who were going to compete in the intellectual and craft events.

'What are we going to do with Frankie during the races?' Pradeep asked.

'It's not like we'll *really* be racing, Pradeep,' I said. 'I can look after him while you're doing your chess-club stuff. And I'm just a reserve for the track team. They'll never make me *actually* race.'

'But are you sure it was a good idea to bring him?' Pradeep went on.

'I couldn't risk leaving Frankie at home,' I replied. 'What if Mark gets home from school before we do? And what about Fang?'

Ever since Mark, my Evil Scientist big brother,

tried to poison Frankie with toxic gunge and flush him down the loo, they've been mortal enemies. It was hard enough having a pet and a big brother who were always trying to attack each other, but things got even worse when Mark got a cute, but totally *evil,* vampire-kitten sidekick called Fang.

Pradeep nodded carefully. He looked a bit green again – probably from the nodding and from looking at the water sloshing about in Frankie's bag. If you hadn't guessed already, Pradeep and bus trips go together like snow and socks, or homework and weekends, or Mark (my Evil Scientist big brother) and Frankie (my pet undead zombie goldfish).

In other words – they don't go together at all.

CHAPTER 2

WHO'S A HOOLIGAN NOW?

'Don't worry, we'll be there soon,' I said to Pradeep. Really I had no idea if we were nearly there or if we were halfway to Timbuktu (not that I know where Timbuktu is, or Timbuk-one, but I'm pretty sure that it's far away).

I rolled up the top of Frankie's bag, stood up and walked a few seats to the front of the bus. 'Mr Thomas?' I leaned over the back of our sports coach's seat. 'Are we nearly there yet?'

'Hunh?' His head jerked as he woke up. Instinctively he turned around to deal with the sound of uproar from the back of the bus. 'Settle down back there,' he bellowed. 'You're

acting like a bunch of hooligans!'

This was Mr Thomas's stock telling-off for any occasion. If you were playing with the Velcro on your shoes during assembly you were 'acting like a bunch of hooligans'. If you were messing around in the dinner line in the cafeteria, you were 'acting like a bunch of hooligans'. If you were attaching rockets to the underbelly of the Earth so that it would shoot off into the sun and blow up into a million pieces and Mr Thomas caught you, he would probably say you were 'acting like a bunch of hooligans'.

I was just picturing what a hooligan might look like when Mr Thomas turned back to me.

'Todd? Tim? Trevor?' He squinted at me.

'Tom,' I replied.

'I knew that,' he said. 'What do you want, kid?' Then he looked over at Pradeep. 'How's the throwing-up boy?'

'Still a bit green, sir,' I explained. 'Are we nearly there yet?'

He looked out of the window. 'We're just arriving. The sports ground's over there.' He pointed to a big field up ahead. 'We'll park in the coach park and head over. Very exciting times for Parkside Primary!' He looked proudly at the hooligans at the back of the bus. Then he looked at me again. 'And you're here because . . . ?'

'I'm on the track team, sir,' I answered. 'I joined last term. I've come last in all the races I've run in so far.' I paused. 'You're my coach, sir.'

'Right,' he said. Then he frowned at Pradeep and the next couple of rows of kids behind him.

There was Susan Church – general-knowledge-quiz champion and expert origami folder, Felix French – Rubik's Cube county champion and winner of the Junior Nobel Prize for Science (for discovering a global cure for nits), Chin Li – multi-language-speaking chess demon and lead violinist in the school orchestra, and Kofi Johnson – mathletics record-holder and winner of *Junior Chef Challenge*. (His strawberry-and-

pomegranate roulade was so good it made the judges *cry*, live on TV.*)*

They were all playing with their calculators.

'And they are here because . . . ?' Mr Thomas went on.

'They're the chess team, sir.' I paused again. 'You don't coach them.'

CHAPTER 3

A LUCKY DAY FOR LOSING

'Right, athletes, listen up!' Mr Thomas called out as I made my way back to my seat. '*Today* is your *lucky* day. You get to represent your school on the playing fields. Run fast, kick or throw that ball into the net, and . . .' He paused and looked at the non-sporty kids. '. . . knit your little socks off, or whatever it is that you do. Let's go out there and win, people!'

The bus erupted into whoops and cheers, especially from the back. Then Mr Thomas added, 'And *TRY* not to act like hooligans!'

'Somehow I don't think today is *my* lucky day,' Pradeep mumbled as he heaved into his bag again.

The coach finally came to a stop and we started to get our stuff together. Our school had made it into the Countywide Inter-Schools Intellectual Sports Day Challenge because we had an ace football team, a championship netball squad and a winning chess team, but all the Parkside Primary teams and clubs had been invited to participate. Other competing schools were coming from across the county and could be primary or secondary schools. In between being sick on the journey, Pradeep had explained that 'the competitors' ages are factored into the scoring system, so that the results accurately reflect the abilities of the kids relative to their age groups'.

When he saw my blank look he'd added, 'Younger kids competing in the same event as older kids will get more points for the same result.'

Every school wanted to win because, besides the gold medals, the winning school would get a *huge* cash prize. If we won, our school was going to put the money towards building a swimming pool. Pradeep and I both thought it would be brilliant! Frankie would finally have somewhere safe to hang out at school. He'd just have to stay out of the way of the swimming team (that is, if we had a swimming team, which we will only have if we build a school pool).

As we were getting off, what looked like a holiday

coach pulled in next to us. The writing on the side said, *St Agnes the Achiever Girls' Preparatory School* and then their school motto in Latin. Chin Li, who speaks seven languages (Mandarin, Cantonese, French, German, Ancient Greek, Latin and Welsh – his mum's from there) translated it for us. It said, 'God wants *us* to win'.

The St Agnes double-decker bus also had a satellite dish on top and what looked like a training room on the lower floor.

'Is that an on-board gym?' Susan Church asked, peering through the windows.

'So they can train on the way?' Pradeep said. 'We're doomed!'

I think I saw Felix French actually wipe a tear from his eye.

'It's OK, guys,' I said. 'None of us lot are even going to compete in the sporting events.'

'Tom's right,' Kofi Johnson said. 'We'll win our chess matches hands down, and maybe even find time to work out a couple more decimal

places for pi while we're cheering on the other Parkside teams.'

Everyone nodded in agreement.

Pradeep nudged me, 'Hey, Tom, I think Mr Thomas is doing roll call for the track team. You'd better get over there.'

'I'll take Frankie, OK?' I said, holding up the sick bag with Frankie inside. Then I noticed that all the chess-club kids were staring at me like I had just said something *really* weird.

'Umm . . . I like to call the different bags names,' I added. 'This one is Frankie.' I patted the bag. 'Come on to the bin then, Frankie.'

CHAPTER 4

JUST A HOP, A FLIP AND A JUMP

Before anyone could say anything, I grabbed my stuff and sped around to the back of the coach. A box of blue team water bottles had been unpacked, and while no one was looking I poured Frankie and the water from the sick bag into a bottle.

'Time to get sporty, Frankie,' I whispered. He looked up at me and then jumped out of the bottle and did a perfect somersault with a triple twist and a wave, before plopping back into the water with barely a splash.

'OK, OK, you're already sporty!' I shook my head. 'I guess it's just me who doesn't belong

here.' I screwed on the lid, put the bottle in my pocket and went to join the super-fit track-team kids for roll call. The fact that I am on the track team *at all* is totally down to my Evil Scientist big brother. One day after school, Mark had managed to kidnap Frankie and was racing home to flush him. Mr Thomas saw me chasing him and made me sign up for the track team right away. Unfortunately I've never run that fast *ever* again. Now I'm stuck on the team until

the end of term, but Mr Thomas has pretty much given up on me. I'm just a reserve, with the job of getting drinks and oranges ready in the breaks.

As soon as roll call was over I went back to the bus and was starting to unload the oranges when I heard a couple of girls from St Agnes talking.

'Camille, make sure that the drinks are *exactly* three degrees above room temperature for the break. That's the optimum level for mineral absorption.' A girl with dark hair pulled back into a tight ponytail and wearing a 'Head Girl' T-shirt was giving orders to another girl with short blonde hair, who was writing it all down in a notepad.

'Cut the oranges exactly five minutes before the break starts so that they are still fresh, refill the water bottles with imported mineral water, fold and warm the towels and prepare the motivational music.'

'Check, check, check, check,' notepad girl said, scribbling away. 'Anything else?'

The head girl looked over at me. 'And *NO* fraternizing with the other teams!' she huffed, glaring at me as she walked away.

I lifted out some more bags of oranges and put them in a cooler to take to the sports ground.

'What does she mean by "no fraternizing"?' I asked.

The blonde girl smiled. 'She means I shouldn't talk to you.' Then she tried to do a glare like the head girl had done, but it just kind of fell off her face and turned into a smile again.

'I'm Camille,' she said.

'I'm Tom,' I replied. 'Are you on orange duty too?'

'Always,' she answered.

'Me too,' I said. 'But I don't mind. I get to eat all the best ones!'

'I want to be out there running,' Camille said, her smile fading, 'but they never give me the chance. I lost my first race at the beginning of term and they won't risk me losing again.'

'You can't *always* win,' I said as we picked up our boxes of oranges and drinks and walked to the sports ground.

'Oh yes you can. And they do.' She paused. 'I don't care about winning though, I just want to race.'

We had just started setting up the break station when Pradeep and the chess team came running across the playing field towards us. That was something I never thought I'd see – the entire chess team breaking into a sweat all at once!

'Tom!' Pradeep panted. 'The other school . . . it's . . . it's . . . Westfield High!'

'Your brother's school!' Kofi Johnson jumped in.

'The third school is Mark's school!' I cried. 'No way!'

'Way indeed,' said Susan Church, rubbing a stitch in her side.

'But . . . there's no way that Mark would actually *be* on any of the teams,' I went on.

'I assure you he is,' Felix French panted.

As I spoke, an eerie 'Mwhaaa haaaaa haaaa haaaaa!' drifted across the playing field. As soon as Frankie heard Mark's evil laugh he started thrashing around so hard in the water bottle that it fell out of my pocket and started rolling towards the sound. Frankie must have been in full-on zombie attack mode in there!

'Mark can't be here!' I cried, dropping to the floor and scrambling after the bottle.

'Oh yes he can!' Pradeep replied.

'Oh *NO* he can't!' Camille repeated. We both gave her a confused look. 'Sorry, I thought it was a panto thing!' She grinned apologetically.

I finally managed to grab the thrashing water

bottle and held on to it tightly to try to stop the shaking. When I looked up, Mark was jogging across the playing field towards us. He was moving really fast, not panting, not sweating and most weirdly of all . . . not complaining about having to do exercise! Normally, unless a sport involved throwing something heavy, he just wasn't interested.

'Hello, morons!' Mark yelled as he got close to the break station. 'Great day to *win*, huh?' He smirked. 'Actually, it's a great day for *me* to win, and it's a great day for *you* to lose!'

CHAPTER 5

AN EVIL WAY TO START THE DAY

Frankie's water bottle was still shaking like mad, so I jumped up and pretended I was using it to do bicep curls. I tried my best to look casual and not to panic.

'Mark!' I forced myself to say. 'What a surprise. Are you competing?'

'That's right, loser,' he said with an evil smile. 'I am representing my track team for the Inter-Schools Smart Arty Sporty Challenge thing.'

'The Inter-Schools Intellectual Sports Day Challenge,' Pradeep corrected him.

Mark scowled. 'Whatever! *My* school are definitely going to win the cash prize, and the person who wins the most events for Westfield High gets to decide what the school spends the money on. And that person will be *ME*! I'm going to have my own personal science lab built, and it won't cost me a penny! Then no one can stop me from doing my . . . *experiments*.' He glared at the chess team, Camille and me. 'So is anyone here gonna put up a fight?' He looked us up and down. 'Nope. Didn't think so.' He

grinned and looked across the playing field at the track, football and netball kids from Parkside Primary. 'I'd better go shake hands with the real competition. See ya, losers!' he yelled over his shoulder as he jogged off.

I shot Pradeep a look that said, 'When did Mark become sporty? Where are the rest of his team?'

Pradeep shot me a look that said, 'I don't know, but I think we have to find out.'

Then Camille shot me a look that said, 'What was all that about? Why are you using a shaking water bottle to do pretend bicep curls? And why are you and your friend talking in secret looks?'

I did a double take as I was not expecting a readable look from Camille.

I took a deep breath and attempted a double look that would say to Camille, 'Ummm, that's my big brother, Mark, who happens to be an Evil Scientist and isn't usually exactly sporty . . . and you're not going to believe this but he and my pet goldfish are mortal enemies so I couldn't let him

know that my fish is in fact in this water bottle.'

And to Pradeep, 'Shoot! She understands our secret looks.'

Camille smiled and said out loud, 'What kind of fish do you have? I keep tropical fish in my spare time.'

'Umm . . . ya know . . . just a goldfish,' I gabbled. Luckily Pradeep pulled me *away* towards the registration tent before I started trying to explain the whole 'zombie goldfish' thing to Camille and the rest of the chess team.

'Yep. Just an *ordinary* goldfish,' Pradeep shouted over his shoulder as we rushed away, which caused Frankie to thrash about even harder.

'Don't be mad, Frankie,' I whispered to the water bottle. 'Pradeep was just trying not to blow your cover.'

'Right,' Pradeep said. 'We can't go around telling people – hey, we have a pet *zombie*

goldfish. You know – the kind with hypnotic powers?'

When we got to the registration tent, the sports coach from Mark's school was inside, explaining to the officials that most of his track team suddenly weren't well enough to compete.

Frankie seemed to have calmed down, so I unscrewed the lid of the bottle and whispered, 'Are you OK?'

Frankie turned his head away and held up a fin in a 'Talk to the fin cos the fish ain't listening' kind of way.

'Come on, Frankie,' Pradeep said.

'You're anything *but* ordinary,' I added. 'You know we know that!'

Frankie finally looked up at us and winked.

I set his water bottle down on an unmanned desk and we walked over to the far side of the tent. Just outside were benches full of track athletes from Mark's school. They were all just sitting there – knitting!

'They must have picked up the needles and wool from the knitting tent,' Pradeep said. 'But why are they all just sitting about?'

'It's as if all their sportiness has been sucked out of them,' I replied. 'But *how*?'

As we headed back to pick up Frankie, we suddenly noticed that Mark's sports coach and all the officials were staring at the side of the tent with one eye and looking up the nostril of the person on their left with the other.

'Swishy little fishy,' Mark's coach mumbled.

'Frankie!' Pradeep whispered, scooping up the water bottle. Frankie popped his head out and looked sheepish.

'Why did you zombify everyone?' I asked.

Frankie pointed a fin at the list of competitors on the table in front of the officials. We walked over to take a closer look. All the track athletes from Mark's school, *except* for Mark, had 'unfit to compete in sports events' written next to their names. Instead of racing, they'd been added to the knitting, group-quilting, cooking, chess and poetry events.

'This definitely proves Mark is up to something,' I muttered. 'Good work, Frankie.'

'But Mark can't be the only one from his school who's racing for the track team, can he?' Pradeep said.

Just then, an announcement came over the loudspeaker. 'Would all competitors please head to their meeting points. The first round of events will begin in ten minutes.'

'We'd better get down to the racetrack to see what Mark is up to,' Pradeep said.

Suddenly a voice behind us boomed, 'Pradeep my lovely! There you are.'

CHAPTER 6

ON YOUR MARKS, GET SET, ZOMBIFY

Walking into the tent behind us was Mrs Kumar, Pradeep's mum, and his three-year-old little sister, Sami.

'Mum! What are you doing here?' Pradeep mumbled.

'I just wanted to make sure you had all your allergy medicines with you!' Mrs Kumar said in a whisper so loud even the kids outside could probably hear what she was saying.

I could tell by the look on Pradeep's face that he was suddenly reliving all of his sports-day disasters at once. You see, Pradeep's allergic to a lot of things (as well as being mega-accident prone), and sports days for him usually end with a trip to the medical tent.

- In Year 4, Pradeep and I managed to get tangled up during the three-legged race and ended up with at least three sprained ankles.

- In Year 3, Pradeep had an allergic reaction to the sack in the sack race and swelled up like a balloon.

- In Year 2, Pradeep had an allergic reaction to the balloon in the balloon toss and swelled up like a watermelon.

- In Year 1, Pradeep had an allergic reaction to the watermelon in the watermelon-rolling race and swelled up like a kid covered in bubble wrap.

- In Reception, Pradeep's mum covered him in bubble wrap under his tracksuit so that he would be protected if he fell over.

Unfortunately Pradeep was immediately swarmed by a herd of kids who knocked him to the ground and spent the rest of the day trying to pop him.

'Race people swishy fishy!' Sami giggled, interrupting the moment.

'Besides, I so wanted to see you compete in the chess tournament,' Mrs Kumar added.

I shot Pradeep a look that said, 'We have to get your mum out of here! Take her to the stands while I get Frankie to unzombify people.'

Pradeep nodded.

Quickly I handed Sami the bottle with Frankie in. Then Pradeep and I grabbed Mrs Kumar and steered her towards the front of the tent.

'Mum, my event isn't for a while yet.' Pradeep smiled his best 'talking to a teacher' smile. 'Why don't you go and watch some other events with Sami while you're waiting?'

'You are so good to your mother!' Pradeep's mum ruffled his hair and called to Sami, 'Come along, little one. Leave those nice people to get on with whatever it is they are doing.'

Sami toddled over and handed back Frankie's bottle. Then she followed Pradeep and Mrs Kumar out of the tent.

'Swishy fishy!' she mumbled as she walked away.

'Did you just zombify Sami too?' I asked Frankie. He shrugged, which is pretty hard to do since goldfish have no shoulders, but somehow he managed it.

'You'll have to unzombify her later,' I said.

'Now unhypnotize this lot, fast!'

As soon as the officials and Mark's sports coach were back to normal, we headed down to the racetrack. Camille was waiting by the break station with her oranges neatly sliced and laid out on china plates, while the St Agnes competitors stood nearby. Mark was at the starting blocks, bouncing on the spot and stretching. It was as if he suddenly had unlimited power and energy.

A few of the best hurdlers from the track team at my school were on the starting blocks too. Unlike Mark, they were looking really bored and were leaning on each other or sitting on the ground. They looked just like the kids from Mark's track team had looked at the registration tent. Like all their sportiness was gone!

Pradeep hurried over, having finally managed to get his mum and Sami to take a seat in the stands. 'Do you think Frankie has zombified the

girls from St Agnes too?' he asked me. 'They look kinda weird.'

Pradeep was right. The St Agnes girls were packed into a huddle, staring as if they were in a trance.

'Frankie?' I whispered into the bottle.

Frankie stayed firmly at the bottom. I handed him to Pradeep and walked up to the St Agnes head girl. 'Are you OK?' I shouted. I stared into her vacant eyes and shook her arm. 'Do you feel you need to stare at a tent and up my left nostril at the same time?' I asked. 'Do you want to say "swishy fishy" over and over again?'

'Urgh!' The head girl pulled her arm out of my grasp. 'Camille, that creepy boy you were talking to is asking me about nostrils and fish. Get him away from me. He's ruined my visualization!' She stormed towards the starting blocks.

Camille came up to me and couldn't resist laughing.

'I ruined her virtualization?' I said.

'Her visualization,' Camille corrected me. 'All the runners visualize the race in their heads before they run it. It's supposed to help them win.'

'I don't think I'd want to tire out my brain and make it run the race twice,' I said. 'That seems a little unfair.'

CHAPTER 7
WINNER TAKES ALL

At that moment, Mark walked up to the St Agnes head girl. 'May the best man win,' he said, holding out his hand.

The head girl looked at Mark's hand and said, 'I don't shake hands. None of us does. Too many germs. Besides, the words I think you were looking for are "May the best *woman* win!"' She turned away and started stretching.

The announcer spoke again. 'Attention. Due to the netball and football teams from St Agnes Preparatory School and Parkside Primary taking naps, playing chess, quilting and reading poetry, Westfield High have won all netball and football

events for the day by default . . . er . . . just for turning up.'

'What?' cried Camille, Pradeep and I at the same time.

'Girls,' shouted the St Agnes head girl, 'we'll just have to make sure we win all the track and intellectual events from now on. We can still win!'

Mark grinned.

'Competitors, please get in place for the following events – hurdles, knitting and poetry,' the announcer went on. 'Feet in the blocks, needles in position and rhymes at the ready.' He laughed at his own joke. 'On your marks . . .'

The track competitors were all in the starting blocks and ready to go.

'Set,' continued the announcer. 'Go!'

The gun sounded and Frankie jumped. If Pradeep hadn't shoved his hand over the top of the bottle he would have gone for Mark right there and then!

The crowd cheered as Mark and the St Agnes girls cleared the first hurdle easily, while the Parkside Primary track team shuffled along behind. A couple of them tried to climb over the first hurdle, one of them ducked under it, and one fell asleep on top of it!

By the third hurdle Mark and the head girl were ahead of everyone else, and in the final sprint the head girl *just* beat him to the line. Another St Agnes girl came third, while the Parkside Primary team seemed to have given up altogether, had found some knitting stuff from

somewhere and had started making a blanket for the sleeping kid.

The first thing Mark did was to go up to the head girl and shake her hand in a sportsmanlike way before she could pull it away. She stared at him for moment and then said, 'I think I need to sit down.'

Camille raced over with her oranges, Pradeep and I trailing behind. She held out the plate of perfectly sliced fruit.

'No, thanks,' the head girl said. She seemed to have found a small volume of poetry from somewhere. 'I don't want my book to get sticky.'

'But . . . you'll need the energy for the next race,' Camille replied.

'I don't really feel like racing any more,' the head girl replied. 'I think I'll just read or take a nap.'

'Something weird is going on here, Pradeep, and Mark is definitely behind it,' I muttered.

'Yeah, the one person that beats Mark is now

suddenly not interested in racing,' Pradeep said. 'That's definitely suspicious.'

Frankie peeked his head out of the water bottle and glared at Mark.

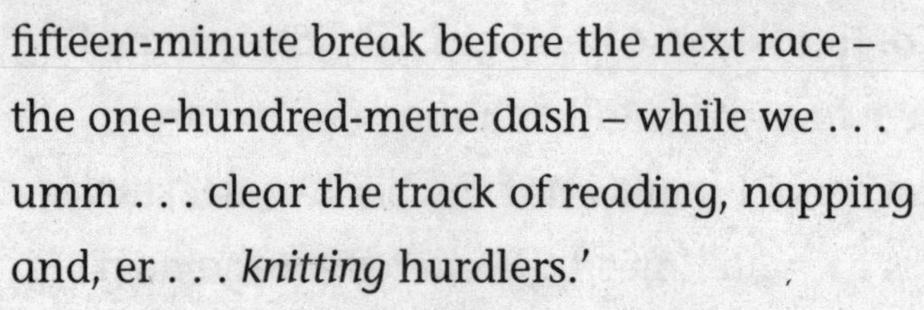

'I know you want to stop him too, Frankie. We just have to figure out how,' I whispered.

The announcer's voice boomed: 'There will be a fifteen-minute break before the next race – the one-hundred-metre dash – while we . . . umm . . . clear the track of reading, napping and, er . . . *knitting* hurdlers.'

In the post-race confusion, we saw Mark slip off towards the parked coaches. He had picked up a small box from his sports bag and was carrying it under one arm.

I shot Pradeep a look that said, 'If we find out what's in that box, we'll find out what Mark's up to!'

'Let's go!' Pradeep's look replied, when our path was suddenly blocked by the St Agnes team coach, wearing a bright red tracksuit with 'Elite Team' embroidered across the front.

'Right,' she yelled as she ran on the spot, 'all of you girls, back to the coach for a pep talk. I've had to switch the netball and football teams to the craft and intellectual events. They're acting very strangely. I think they must have caught some kind of bug. Germs, that's the problem. What do I always tell you, girls?'

The St Agnes girls chanted, 'Germs on faces lose us races, germs on hands keep us sitting in the stands.'

'Exactly!' The St Agnes coach nodded and switched to star jumps. 'So now it's up to you to WIN!' She pointed to the head girl. 'Somebody move her to the spectator stands so she's out of the way! Spit, spot, girls. Let's go!'

With that she led the way back to their bus,

Camille and the other girls following behind. That's when I noticed Mark was back on the sports field, but this time without the box.

CHAPTER 8

WINNERS CAN'T BE CHOOSERS

At that moment, Mr Thomas strode towards us. 'Tylor? Tony? Tarquin?' He pointed at me.

'Tom,' I said. 'You could just call me "Hey, you", sir, if that's easier.'

'Right,' he said. 'You have to run in this race.'

'I . . . I . . . I can't!' I stammered. 'What about the netball team?'

'I've reassigned them to the cookery event,' he said. 'They're practising their soufflés.'

'The football team?' I pleaded.

'They've made themselves pyjamas and are

finishing the quilt they're sewing. The quilting judging is coming up and they have to "get their borders nice and pretty",' he huffed.

I gulped.

'You're the only one left on *any* sports team who's not reading, knitting, napping or playing chess. You *have* to do the race.' Mr Thomas patted me on the back.

Pradeep looked over at me. 'You can do it, Tom!' his look said.

I can't do it! I wanted to scream. I wanted to tell him that it was hopeless, that we might as well go home now and let Mark and his school win. I wanted to convince him with some kind of Jedi mind trick – *I am not the runner you are looking for!* I wanted to sneak back to the bus and hide, but instead for some reason I said, 'OK,' and headed off towards the starting blocks. I knew that I couldn't run just for the sake of it, *even* if it meant beating Mark. I shook myself anyway and did some pretend stretching. I knew

I wasn't going to win, but at least I could try so that my team didn't feel too let down.

'Competitors, please take your places for the next events,' the announcer's voice echoed. 'Quilting – judging in the yellow tent. Chess tournament – this will take place in the blue tent. Cookery – in the refreshments tent. One-hundred-metre dash – please make your way to the racetrack!'

I put my feet in the blocks in the lane next to Mark's and crouched down.

He looked at me. 'Loser,' he mouthed.

'Good luck, Tom!' called Pradeep, who'd joined me at the starting line. He put Frankie's water bottle down and gave me a thumbs-up. Then he headed off to the blue tent.

'Where are the competitors from the St Agnes team?' the race official standing on the starting line shouted. Everyone looked around, but there was no sign of the girls from St Agnes anywhere.

'Last call for St Agnes runners,' said the

announcer over the loudspeaker.

We waited for a few more minutes, but no one appeared.

'We can't hold off any longer,' said the starting official. 'Runners in position.' He held the starting pistol over his head and pointed it up and away from us.

'Ready . . . set . . . go!'

The gun fired and I watched in what seemed like slow motion as a flash of orange flew past me. I looked back over my shoulder and saw a zombified Sami holding a slingshot.

Frankie! my brain screamed.

My pet zombie goldfish was flying through the air straight towards the finishing line. If I didn't

get there before he came down he'd be splatted on the track! The power surged through my legs as I pushed off the blocks and started to build up speed, my eyes on the flash of orange ahead of me. Mark had spotted the flying fish too and pulled ahead, but I couldn't let him stop me! Somewhere deep inside I found the strength to push harder. I caught up with Mark and then overtook him.

I could hear the crowd cheering and Mr Thomas yelling, 'Come on, what's-his-name!' but I didn't care. I just had to get to Frankie.

As we neared the finish line, the orange dot that was Frankie was almost close enough to grab. But I wasn't fast enough. I'd have to dive to save him!

CHAPTER 9

SWISHY FISHY FINISH

With less than a metre to go, I threw myself forward with my hands outstretched. Mark raced past me and crossed the line as I skidded along the gravel track and felt the wet squelch of goldfish landing safely in my hands.

Mark stood in front of me and punched the air. His sports coach came up to him.

'Amazing run, Mark. You're the fastest athlete here by far. Keep it up, lad, and not only will our school win the competition, but *you'll* get to choose what we spend the money on!'

Mr Thomas came over just as I was picking myself up off the floor. 'That was the fastest I've

ever seen you run, kid. But what happened at the end? I thought you had that race in the bag.'

'In the bag,' Sami repeated, having somehow toddled to the finishing line already. For a three-year-old, she can be scarily speedy! 'Swishy fishy bag,' she said, and slipped Frankie from my cupped hands into a sick bag filled with water. One of her eyes was looking up Mr Thomas's left nostril and the other at the spectators.

'Have I got something on my face?' Mr Thomas asked Sami.

'Swishy fishy,' she replied.

While Mr Thomas went off to check for bits of fish on his face and Mark was busy being congratulated, I opened the bag and whispered to Frankie, 'I know what you were trying to do – but you could've got hurt!'

Frankie waved a fin in a 'Naaaaah!' kind of way.

'Seriously!' I said. 'And can you unzombify Sami now and get her back to Mrs Kumar, OK?'

Frankie nodded. I picked up an empty dark blue water bottle from Mr Thomas's kit bag and quickly poured him inside, then I handed it to Sami and she started to toddle back towards the stands.

Just then Mark strode over to me and held out his hand.

'Good race, moron . . . I mean . . . um, Tom,' he said. And he smiled an evil smile and grabbed my hand. Then he leaned in and whispered, 'I know you've got your stupid fish helping you – but I'll take care of that. I will win EVERY race. I will get my Evil Science lab. And when I do . . . you'll be sorry! Mwah haaaa haaaa haaa ha!'

'That's what I like to see. Good sportsmanship,' muttered a race official as he walked by. 'Although that *is* a slightly creepy laugh.'

The next thing I remember was Pradeep's worried face looking down at me. We appeared to be off the track, over by the spectator stands. 'Tom, are you OK?' he asked.

'How'd the chess match go?' I said, and yawned.

'Checkmate in seven moves!' Pradeep grinned, but then he looked worried again. 'Are you sure you're feeling OK? You don't look so good.'

I felt this overwhelming need to have a snooze, and then maybe sew something. Or knit. Knitting sounded good. I was suddenly so drained. Then it hit me. Drained, I was *drained.* And it was Mark who had drained me.

'Pradeep, it's the handshake,' I whispered as I lay back on the floor. 'Mark's handshake. That's how he's draining the sportiness from everyone.'

Pradeep looked up at the St Agnes head girl, still happily reading poetry in the spectator stands next to us.

'You're right!' Pradeep said. 'He shook hands with the head girl, *and* with everyone on our track team before the first race.'

'He must have shaken hands with our football and netball teams earlier, the St Agnes teams . . . and even the track team from his own school too!' I added sleepily.

Just then Camille came running in from the parking lot. 'Tom, are you OK?' she cried.

'I've lost all my sportiness,' I replied.

'I didn't know you had any,' she said with a smile.

'My Evil Scientist big brother, Mark, is somehow sucking out people's sportiness with his handshake!' I explained.

'What?' cried Camille. 'That's terrible!'

'We've got to figure out how to reverse this,' Pradeep butted in. 'If Mark can use the handshake to drain people's sportiness, there's got to be a way to get it back.'

'But why weren't *all* of the St Agnes track team affected?' I thought out loud.

'Most of them managed *not* to shake hands with Mark,' Camille said. 'Too many germs, remember?'

'So where are they then?' Pradeep asked.

'Locked in the school bus,' Camille said. 'That's what I was coming to tell you. We were heading into the gym when one of the girls spotted this little kitten on its own in a box by the bus. When she went to pick it up, the kitten ran into the bus

and upstairs to the changing rooms. Everyone, including the sports coach, kept shrieking about how cute it was and followed it.'

'Did the kitten have strangely long front teeth,' I murmured, 'that looked a bit like . . . ?'

'Fangs?' Camille, Pradeep and I said at the same time.

CHAPTER 10

THROWING FOR GOLD

'Fang used her power of cuteness to lure the girls on to the top deck of the bus,' Pradeep said, shaking his head. 'Will that evil kitten stop at nothing?'

'I'm not really into cute furry things,' Camille said. 'That's why I didn't bother going up. I much prefer tropical fish. Once they were all up there, the kitten slipped out through their legs, ran through the door, kicked it closed and somehow jumped up and grabbed the key! She ran off with it in her mouth.'

'That's pretty impressive,' I said, finding a more comfortable position on the grass.

'Even if it *is* completely evil!'

'I've spent the last twenty minutes trying to pick the lock,' Camille went on, 'but it's no good. And the emergency exit is blocked by gym equipment. They're really stuck in there. Plus, it looks as if I missed the hundred-metre dash!' she added, and scuffed the gravel with her trainer.

'The next event – the javelin throw – is about to start. Will the competitors please take their places on the playing field?' the announcer boomed over the loudspeaker. 'Speed-knitting finalists, please head to the blue tent. Round two of the poetry challenge will be in the yellow tent.'

'We can't let Mark win . . .' I whispered to Pradeep and Camille. 'Or he'll get to build his Evil Science lab, and then he'll be . . . well . . . even *MORE* evil . . .' I trailed off.

'Tom!' Pradeep shook me awake. 'What are we going to do? There's no one sporty left!'

'You have to do it,' I mumbled. 'You have to throw the javelin, Pradeep.'

By now, the rest of the chess-club kids had arrived, and while they helped me into a seat

in the spectator stands closest to the throwing circle, Camille grabbed Pradeep by the arm and dragged him down to choose a javelin. I looked around hopefully in case someone had left some half-finished knitting nearby, but no one had.

Camille was first. She got into position, pulled back her arm and threw with all her might. The javelin flew a good way before it landed. The officials went out to mark her distance and then Pradeep was up.

Pradeep looked back at me as he stood on the

dirt circle. 'I really don't think today can get any worse,' his look said.

'Pradeep!' The shout of shame echoed across the field. 'Coooooeee! It's Mummy.'

'Or maybe it could,' Pradeep's look added.

'I just want to check that the javelin has been cleaned properly,' Mrs Kumar shouted. 'I have antibacterial wipes!'

CHAPTER 11
CHOMPING A CHAMPION

Sami skipped along after Pradeep's mum, who was bustling towards the throwing circle, waving her wet wipes.

'Hi, Tom!' Sami waved at me as they went past. 'Me got swishy fishy!' She held up the water bottle and I suddenly had a brilliant idea.

'Sami!' I yelled. 'Can you give the bottle to Pradeep?'

While Pradeep's mum wiped down the javelin, Pradeep's hands and the official's hands with her antibacterial wipes, Sami handed her big brother the water bottle.

I saw Pradeep peek inside, then pat Sami on

the head and set the bottle down next to him in the circle. Mrs Kumar planted an especially embarrassing kiss on Pradeep's head, handed Pradeep the spotless javelin and then led Sami back to the stands.

It was time for Pradeep to take his throw. Just as the javelin was about to leave his hand . . . Frankie launched himself out of the bottle in a blur of orange and chomped Pradeep square on the bum, before plopping back into the water with a splash!

'YaaaaaaaAAAaawwwwwwwwwwwhhhhhh!'

Pradeep yelled as he hurled the javelin with more force than I had ever seen Pradeep hurl anything.

The officials measured the throw while Pradeep rubbed his bottom. 'Thanks, Frankie,' I could see him saying. And, 'Ouch!'

Incredibly, the distance was a straight tie with Camille's throw! Now there was only Mark left to go. As he walked up to the throwing spot, he grinned and said something to Pradeep that looked like, 'Nice shot, moron. Let me shake your hand to congratulate you,' but Pradeep wrapped both his hands around the water bottle and backed away.

Mark started to prepare for his throw . . . and that's when I noticed the little furry tail sticking out from the hood of his sweatshirt. It had to be Fang! Maybe she still had the key to the coach and we could get the girls from St Agnes out?

I dragged myself out of my seat and started to

move towards the throwing area so I could warn Pradeep.

Just as Mark was about to let go of the javelin, a shot of orange sprang from the water bottle in Pradeep's hands, bounced off the throwing circle and landed in the hood of Mark's sweatshirt.

'Frankie!' I croaked, speeding up.

Mark lurched, distracted by the wrestling match taking place in his hood – and his javelin went high, landing in exactly the same place as Pradeep's and Camille's.

He yanked his thrashing hoodie over his head. 'Moron fish!' I could just hear him whining. 'You ruined my throw!

He ducked into an empty officials' tent at the edge of the throwing area while the officials measured his distance, and I noticed that he was closely followed by Sami, who had somehow escaped from Mrs Kumar's watchful gaze.

'Bad kitty. Bad fishy. No fighting!' I could hear her shouting.

By the time Pradeep, Camille and I made it to the tent, Mark had dropped the thrashing sweatshirt and was nursing a scratched thumb.

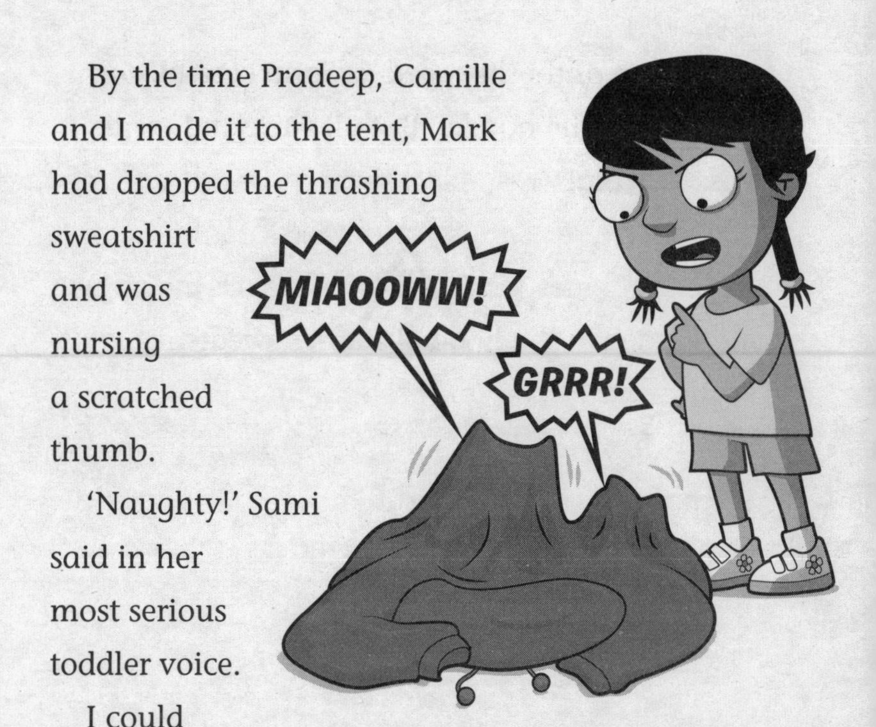

'Naughty!' Sami said in her most serious toddler voice.

I could hear a muted 'Miaoowww!' from Fang and an apologetic but muffled 'Grrr!' from Frankie.

'Play nice,' Sami said sternly to the hoodie, which immediately stopped shaking.

'How does the little moron do that?' Mark asked.

'Is she *really* talking to . . . a kitten and a fish?' asked Camille.

Pradeep and I shrugged as Sami carefully unwrapped the hoodie. But all we found inside was . . . Fang!

CHAPTER 12

COOL ZOMBIE RUNNINGS

'Frankie!' Pradeep and I yelled at the same time.

'Drop fishy,' Sami said in her cute but serious toddler voice. 'Now!'

With a splutter, Fang spat out Frankie and Pradeep quickly scooped him up and put him back into the water bottle. His gills flapped gently, then he opened his glowing green eyes and tried to launch himself straight back out!

Pradeep quickly shoved his hand over the top of the bottle. 'It isn't worth it!' he whispered to Frankie.

'Come on, evil kitty,' Mark snapped. 'Let's make sure we win this thing.' Then he grabbed

Fang, covered her with his hoodie and stormed back on to the field.

The loudspeaker crackled into life. 'We have combined the points from all the sporting and intellectual events and we can now announce . . .' There was a pause during which you could hear bits of paper being shuffled around. '. . . there is a tie between all three schools!'

The crowd in the stands muttered excitedly.

'We will take a short break to reset the track for the final event. This will be an obstacle race that will incorporate all the elements of the day! Please choose *TWO* competitors from each school. The race will start in thirty minutes!'

'Now's our chance,' Pradeep said. 'We've got to find out how Mark is sapping people's sportiness with his handshake and then figure out how to reverse the process.'

'And we've got to free the St Agnes track team!' Camille added. 'Is your fish OK? It looked like . . . well . . . it looked like its eyes were glowing, and that it was trying to fight that evil kitten. But . . .'

She was interrupted by a sound from the water bottle like a fish clearing a hairball followed by a very loud BUUUURP! Frankie had coughed up a shining silver key! He popped his head out of the top and held it up to Camille.

'Rude fishy,' Sami giggled.

'That's no *ORDINARY* goldfish,' Camille gasped.

Frankie winked and splashed back into the bottle.

'Actually he's a zombie goldfish,' I admitted. 'It's a bit of a long story.'

'He must have wrestled the key off Fang and swallowed it for safe keeping while they were fighting!' Pradeep said. 'Nice one, Frankie!'

At that moment the chess-club kids arrived. 'There you are!' said Felix French.

'What's going on?' asked Chin Li.

'Is it something evil?' asked Kofi Johnson.

'How can we help?' said Susan Church.

'Mark has been draining people's sportiness by using his handshake,' explained Pradeep. 'Yes, it's evil, and yes, we need your help. Tom and Camille – you free the St Agnes track team. The rest of us will figure out the chemistry behind Mark's evil powers!' He handed the water bottle to Sami. 'You look after Frankie,' he added in a whisper. 'Go and find Mum – she'll be looking for you.'

Felix spoke up. 'I've got my junior chemistry set in my sports bag!' he said. 'I never leave home without it. If we do a litmus test on Mark's palm, then we should be able to analyse whatever he's using to sap people's sportiness, replicate it and come up with a compound to counteract it.'

'Translation?' I said to Pradeep.

'We'll see what it's made of, make more and produce an antidote,' Pradeep answered.

'That's what *I* said,' Felix mumbled.

Camille and I headed to the coach park, but I was so drained the most I could manage was a fast walk. By the time we got there, the girls were using practice javelins to try to pry open the windows so they could squeeze out.

'Hang on!' Camille yelled up! 'We've managed to get the key back!' She opened the door and the girls poured downstairs, muttering, 'Thank you,' and insisting they'd never trust kittens again.

'Right, girls, let's hustle,' their sports coach

snapped, stretching against the side of the bus. 'From what I heard the announcer say on the loudspeakers, we can still win this thing! Good work, Camille. Girls, let's GO!'

CHAPTER 13

THE SCIENCE OF SPORT

By the time we'd run (Camille) and shuffled (me) back to the officials' tent, the chess club's science experiments were in full swing.

Pradeep filled us in from his position lounging on the grass. 'I had to go and get Mark to shake my hand with the litmus paper hidden in my palm.' He knitted as he spoke. 'It had to be me – I was the only kid left at

Parkside Primary that Mark would want to suck any sportiness from.'

'It worked though,' Felix French interrupted. 'We've isolated the compound and copied it already.' He held up some light blue goo. 'Mark has created an ingenious chemical gel that absorbs the sportiness of an individual through their pores! This stuff is *so* strong it will override Mark's compound and suck all the sportiness straight out of him!'

'That's great!' I said, fighting off the urge to grab Pradeep's knitting and have a go.

'Hang on though. If the compound just drains sportiness, how are we going to give it back to everyone he took it from?' asked Camille.

'By making an antidote gel,' Susan Church interrupted.

'And we can do that?' I asked.

'Of course,' Susan replied. 'Well, we could if we had the right ingredients. It's just a shame that we don't have anything acidic such as citrus

fruits to make the chemical compound.'

'Citrus fruits?' I said.

Then Camille and I looked at each other. 'Oranges!' we cried. 'We've got oranges!'

Within minutes the chess club had managed to prepare an antidote, while Pradeep and I knitted a lovely cover for Frankie's water bottle.

There were only four minutes left before the start of the race when Kofi Johnson finally said, 'We're ready!'

His right hand was smeared with blue goo – ready to take all Mark's stolen sportiness – and his left hand had been covered in orange goo – so he could transfer sportiness back to the 'drained' athletes.

He marched across the playing field to where Mark was waiting at the starting line for the final event. 'Good luck,' Kofi said, and held out his blue-goo smeared hand.

'Good luck, moron,' I heard Mark reply, followed by an evil 'Mwah haaaa haaaa ha!'

as he grabbed Kofi's hand.

At that moment Chin Li ran up to the two of them with a digital camera. 'Hold that pose,' he said. 'For the school paper!' Then he started taking about a zillion photos.

'Hurry up!' Mark muttered. 'The race is about to start!'

'All done!' called Chin after a minute, and both chess-club kids ran straight back. Well, Kofi sprinted, and Chin sort of bumbled.

'Did it work?' cried Susan.

'I think so,' said Kofi. 'I feel *amazing*! But I didn't have time to suck *all* the sportiness back. We'll have to try again after the race!' He grabbed my left hand with his orange-smeared hand, and I could feel a surge of energy run up my arms and down into my legs. It worked!

Kofi gripped Pradeep's hand too, using the orange antidote, and then raced over to the St Agnes head girl, who was now embroidering a quilt in the stands. He grabbed her with his orange-goo-covered hand and pulled her up.

'Competitors for the final obstacle race, please take your places on the track,' the announcer's voice boomed over the speakers.

Mark had been joined by his sports coach and

one of the star sprinters from his school at the starting line. The sprinter tripped over his feet as he tried to get into the blocks.

'Why does he have to race with me?' Mark was whining. 'I could totally do this on my own.'

'You're doing great, Mark,' the coach said, helping up the other runner, 'but Jezza here did a lovely meringue in the cooking challenge and recited a very moving Shakespeare sonnet in the poetry event. We need both of you out there to win.'

The St Agnes head girl had reached the starting line too and was warming up. Her coach jogged over, whispered something into her ear and then beckoned to Camille. 'You've done great today, kid.' The coach slapped her on the back. 'I think it's time we gave you a second chance!'

Camille grinned over at us as she got into the starting blocks.

Just then, Mr Thomas came up to the officials' tent and patted me and Pradeep on the shoulders. 'How are my little track stars today?' he asked.

We both looked around to see who he was talking to.

'I mean you two,' he said. 'You have to represent Parkside Primary in this race. We need you, Preston and Trey!'

'It's Pradeep and Tom,' I corrected him.

'B . . . b . . . but there's gotta be some other people that could do this,' Pradeep stuttered.

'You're our only hope,' Mr Thomas said as he dragged us towards the starting line.

'The rules of the race are simple,' the announcer said over the loudspeaker. 'This is an obstacle course made up of race sections and

stations. *Both* competitors have to make it to each station. At least *one* competitor from each school needs to do the activity at each station before you can move on.'

'On your marks, get set . . .'

Then the starting pistol sounded and we were off.

CHAPTER 14

FRANKIE, CHAMPION OF THE WORLD

The first one hundred metres was hurdles. We all took off quickly out of the blocks.

It's fair to say that Pradeep and I didn't *technically* clear any of the hurdles, but we managed to stumble over them somehow. Mark was racing well – he still had lots of stolen sportiness in him – but Jezza was struggling and falling behind.

Camille and the St Agnes head girl stormed ahead to the first station. It was a cooking challenge. The task: to make an elegant fruit salad!

Mark had arrived and was hacking away

randomly at a pineapple. Camille was already chopping oranges, apples and mangoes like a pro. As we crawled over the last hurdle and sprinted towards the station, I suddenly spotted Pradeep's first potential sports-day disaster.

'Don't touch the watermelons!' I screamed, and I threw myself in front of Pradeep. 'I'll make the fruit salad!' I started chopping away next to Camille. 'See?' I said. 'All that orange chopping was really race training in disguise.' She smiled.

Jezza finally caught up with everyone else. He might have lost his running ability, but his cooking skills were awesome. He whipped the pineapple away from Mark and created a delicious exotic fruit salad in moments!

'Later, morons,' yelled Mark, as his team and Camille's set off.

I was just pouring my salad into a presentation dish when Pradeep grabbed my arm. 'Tom . . . it's a sack race next! I can't do it . . . I'm sorry!'

I looked at the sacks. Then I looked at Pradeep. I could see he was imagining himself swelling up like a balloon. 'Don't worry, Pradeep, I've got a plan!' I said. I jumped into a sack and pulled it up to my waist. 'Climb on my back,' I yelled. 'I'll hop us to the next station.'

As I hopped as best I could, the others arrived at the next station and started playing chess against a computer, but both teams were losing fast. I huffed my final few hops to the station and collapsed on the floor, while Pradeep sat down at the computer. Five moves later he was

pulling me up for the next leg of the race. 'We're in the lead now,' he yelled. 'I don't believe it!'

We looked out at the stands as we ran the sprint section of the race. Pradeep's mum was clapping – while Sami had toddled down to the side of the track and was waving Frankie's bottle at us from near the finishing line. The chess team were screaming and cheering, and I could see a huge banner that the football, netball and track teams had knitted for us. It read, 'GO, TOM AND PRADEEP, GO!' Camille's team was right behind us now, closely followed by Mark and Jezza as we all approached the poetry station.

Jezza recited his Shakespeare sonnet to one judge there, while the head girl spoke a poem she had written herself.

I was just about to launch into a limerick that I had once read in a greetings card when Pradeep stepped forward and started reciting

a poem about trees that he had used for our school-play auditions earlier in the year.

We all finished at just about the same time. There was one short dash left to the finish, but just as we were about to start running, the judges handed out thick rubber bands to each pair. It was a three-legged sprint!

Camille and the head girl were the first to set off and seemed to move perfectly in time.

Mark and Jezza were next, but Mark kept shouting at Jezza to keep up with him, throwing off their pace.

Pradeep looked at me. 'The last time we did this we both ended up with sprained ankles,' he said.

'I know,' I replied, 'but if it happens again, at least this time we can knit each other really cool ankle supports.' I smiled at him. 'We can do this.'

Pradeep and I set off, shouting, 'Middle, out, middle, out, middle, out . . .' so we knew which

legs to move and when. I think we had got in a muddle last time by saying, 'Left, right . . .'

We overtook Mark and Jezza and were gaining on Camille and her teammate.

'Middle, out, middle, out . . .' We got faster and faster and soon we were just ahead of Camille's team. Pradeep and I were *finally* going to win something and neither of us had ended up in the medical tent!

We were steps away from the finishing line.

That's when it happened.

Sami was still standing near the edge of the track with Frankie in his water bottle. Frankie was peeping out, punching the air with a fin and cheering us on. His eyes weren't glowing, which meant his zombie-fish danger senses couldn't tell he was in trouble.

But he was.

On the edge of the awning above the spectator stands was Fang. She was poised, bottom wriggling, ready to pounce.

'Pradeep, look!' I shouted, instead of 'Middle'.

'No, Frankie!' Pradeep shouted back instead of 'Out'.

Fang licked her lips, then leaped through the air.

CHAPTER 15

A FATAL FISHY FINISH?

We didn't even have to think. It was as if time had slooooooooowed down. Turning away from the finishing line, we threw ourselves off the track towards Sami and Frankie! Rolling in mid-air so we both landed on our backs, I grabbed Sami, who was still clutching tightly to Frankie's water bottle, while Fang crash-landed on Pradeep's

stomach and bounced off in the other direction.

At the same moment, the St Agnes team crossed the line just in front of Mark and Jezza.

'Nooooooo!' Mark was shrieking. 'It's not fair! I should have won. ME! IT'S NOT FAIR!'

We sat up and dusted ourselves off, while Fang hissed and shot Frankie a look. If I could read cat looks I would swear she said, 'You were lucky this time, fishy, but we will meet again!'

Frankie was trying to wriggle out of the bottle and turn his zombie stare on her, but Fang quickly turned her face away and bounded over to hide in Mark's sports bag.

Mrs Kumar came rushing through the crowd, checked Sami quickly for cuts and bumps, and then threw herself at Pradeep.

'My lovely, are you all right? Did you bang your head? How many fingers am I holding up? Do you know what county we're in? Can you remember the twelve times table?' She moved a finger from side to side in front of his eyes.

I realized that the only one of those questions I could possibly answer was the finger one.

'I'm fine!' Pradeep said. 'Really, I'm OK.'

Pradeep's mum gave him that mum look that means, 'Are you sure?'

Pradeep sighed. 'Twelve, twenty-four, thirty-six, forty-eight, sixty, seventy-two,' he rattled off. She hugged him and simultaneously checked his head for bumps. Then she moved on to me.

'Tom, are you all right?' she started. 'Thank you for getting Sami out of the way! She could have been scratched . . . or worse!'

I pulled away as I answered her so she couldn't start checking my head too. 'I'm OK too, Mrs Kumar. Thanks. We're fine, really. Why don't you take a seat for the prize presentations?'

'If you're sure,' she said doubtfully.

'We're sure,' Pradeep and I said at the same time.

Sami handed me the water bottle and took

her mum's hand. 'Bye-bye,' she said, pulling her mum away.

The announcer's voice crackled over the loudspeaker again. 'That was an exciting finale to our competition!' he said, and everyone in the stands cheered. 'All three schools competed very well. The judges wanted me to especially congratulate Westfield High School for their achievements in the sprint, knitting and cooking areas, St Agnes Prep for their skills in poetry, quilting and hurdles, and Parkside Primary for their javelin and chess success.'

The crowd cheered again.

'Could I please have *all* the teams – sporting, craft and intellectual – on the field for the final announcement of the winner!'

'Let's get moving,' Mr Thomas bellowed automatically at the Parkside kids. 'And try not to act like a bunch of . . .' He trailed off. 'Er . . . poetry-reading hooligans. Let's go!'

Mark, Jezza and the other members of

Westfield High (knitting needles and quilts still in hand) slowly headed down to the field. Mark shot us a look that could have said, 'This is sooo your fault, morons. I'm gonna get you and your stupid fish!' Or it could have said, 'That tracksuit is sooo your colour, Tom. I'm gonna get one just like it but with a fish!'

Sometimes it's hard to read his looks.

Camille and the other St Agnes girls headed past us as well, with their sports coach. Camille smiled as she went past. 'It's a shame you had to lose the race, but I know it was worth it to save a friend,' her look said.

We smiled back and then looked down at Frankie, who'd calmed down now. When no one was looking, he jumped up and high-fived first me and then Pradeep.

'You're welcome, Frankie,' I said as we started to walk towards the field.

'Tom? Pradeep?' a voice interrupted us. It was Mr Thomas. 'Good job out there, boys.' He patted us on the back. 'Shame you had to make a dive to save that little girl from being clawed by some kind of wild kitten – but you did great! You should be proud of yourselves.'

'Thanks,' I replied in surprise, giving Pradeep a look that said, 'Did he just get our names right?'

The announcer's voice broke through the murmurings of the crowd. 'The winner, by a very small margin, of this year's Countywide Inter-Schools Intellectual Sport's Day Challenge is . . .'

CHAPTER 16

WORTH THE WAIT

The St Agnes head girl reached over and grabbed Camille's hand. Mark glared at us, and even the Parkside Primary kids seemed to be holding their breath . . .

'St Agnes the Achiever Preparatory School for Girls!'

Suddenly the whole of the St Agnes team was a mob of bouncing ponytails, hugging each other, crying and giggling at the same time.

'I SO don't get girls,' Pradeep whispered.

Mark stomped his foot and muttered, 'Stupid morons, stupid fish, stupid sports day!'

The St Agnes team went up on the podium to

collect their trophy and have their picture taken, and Camille and the head girl were handed a microphone.

'It's great to win,' Camille said, 'but it's great to share this prize with friends too.'

'All the teams from all the schools worked really hard today, and we are *all* winners,' the head girl added.

'And what are you going to do with the prize money for your school?' an official asked.

The head girl nodded at Camille, who answered, 'We really want the school to have a

tropical fish tank installed so we can learn about the care and behaviour of exotic fish. They're SO much more interesting than kittens!'

The rest of the St Agnes students murmured in agreement.

Camille smiled over at me and Frankie, who was peeking out of his bottle. 'After all, some fish behaviour has to be seen to be believed!'

'There is one more special prize that we would like to give out today,' the official said, taking back the microphone, 'which is the prize for team spirit. Could Tom and Pradeep from Parkside Primary please come up to the winners' podium to accept their award?'

Pradeep looked at me and I looked at Pradeep, but the only thing readable in either of our looks was, *'WOW!'*

We headed up to the platform and were handed a silver trophy, to the cheers of the crowd.

'Ummmm . . .' I spoke into the microphone.

'There are other people that deserve to share this trophy too. Without them we wouldn't be here.'

Pradeep spoke up. 'This award also belongs to the Parkside Primary chess team, Camille from St Agnes and my little sister, Sami!'

I looked down into the water bottle and whispered. 'And you too, Frankie!'

As the crowd cheered, Pradeep tugged on my arm. He shot me a look that said, 'This is great and everything, but how are we going to get Mark to give back all the sportiness he sucked out of everyone?'

Just then I spotted Mr Thomas walking up to the sports coach from Mark's school and shaking his hand. I nudged Pradeep so he saw them too.

'I think I have an idea,' I said.

CHAPTER 17

IN WITH A SPORTING CHANCE

As we walked back down into the crowd, we knew exactly what we had to do.

'We need to get Mark to shake the hands of everyone he stole sportiness from,' Pradeep thought out loud. 'So that's his own track team, the St Agnes football and netball teams, and pretty much all the Parkside Primary sports teams.'

'It's only sportsmanlike,' I added with a smile. 'Plus, if we can make sure he has the orange antidote goo on his hands, then he'll give back their sportiness without even knowing he's doing it!'

We found the chess team and explained our plan, and then Pradeep and I rounded up Mr Thomas and Mark's sports coach and brought them over to where Mark was standing.

'Mark,' I practically yelled. Some of the race officials looked over too as I was speaking so loudly. 'I told the sports coaches what you said . . . about wanting to be a good sport and show your track teammates *and* the other teams that there were no hard feelings.'

'Hunh?' Mark gave me an evil stare. 'What are you talking about?'

'Very sportsmanlike of you, young man,' Mr Thomas said.

Mark's sports coach nodded. 'Great,' he said. 'Let's get a handshake line going!'

'What?' Mark mumbled.

Within minutes, Pradeep, Susan, Kofi and Chin had picked out all the kids that Mark had drained and had them standing in a long line.

Just before Mark was about to start shaking hands, Frankie started thrashing about like crazy in the bottle I was holding and splashed water all over him!

'You moron!' yelled Mark, wiping his hands on his shorts and also wiping off the last traces of his sport-sapping compound.

'Whoops!' I said, looking at the sports coaches who were still standing nearby. 'I must have tripped and splashed you.'

Mark glared at me as Felix French, the first kid in the queue, walked up and grabbed Mark's hand with a squelch.

'Urgh!' Mark pulled back, looking at his dripping, orange hand.

'It's just hand gel,' said Felix, 'to protect you from germs.' He winked at me as he walked away, wiping his hands clean with a towel.

Pradeep and I watched as Mark shook hands with every single kid in the queue. By the end he was so exhausted he could barely walk back to the track to pick up his sports bag, which contained one very annoyed evil kitten.

He glared across the field at me and Pradeep, and Fang stuck her head out of the bag and glared at us too. 'I'll get you morons for this, you and your stupid fish!' their evil looks said. Mark added a feeble, 'Mwhaaa haa ha ha!' and Fang ended her look with an evil, 'Miaow, miaow, miaow, miaow, miaow,' just to make sure we got the message.

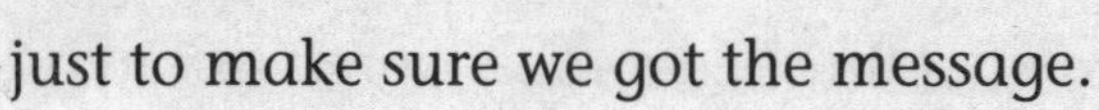

*

Even though everyone got their sportiness back, as the kids piled on to their different school coaches to go home some of them were still knitting or clutching poetry books.

'Do you think the antidote didn't work on them?' I asked Pradeep, holding the bottle with Frankie inside as we walked back to our bus.

'Naaah.' Pradeep shrugged. 'I think they just realized that they liked doing that stuff too.'

Camille came over to say goodbye. Frankie popped his head out of his water bottle and she gently stroked his gills. 'You can come and visit St Agnes any time,' she said to him. 'Especially when we have the fish tank. Just be nice to the other fish, OK?' Then she waved at Pradeep and me as she bounded on to the bus with the other girls.

'You know, Pradeep,' I said, 'even though our school didn't win so we won't get a school pool, for once sports day wasn't *all* that bad. You drew in a javelin toss, *almost* finished a race, won a trophy and returned sportiness to dozens of athletes!'

Pradeep smiled. 'You're right. Maybe my sports-day trips to the medical tent are finally over.' He started to walk around the back of the bus to get to the door on the far side.

'Maybe today *is* your lucky day after all,' I added.

THIS FISH JUST GOT NASTY!

When Tom's big brother dunks Frankie the goldfish into toxic green gunge, Tom zaps the fish with a battery to bring him back to life! But there's something weird about the new Frankie – he's now a BIG FAT ZOMBIE GOLDFISH with hypnotic powers . . . and he's out for revenge.

HE'S BACK . . .
AND BADDER THAN EVER!

Frankie is a BIG FAT ZOMBIE GOLDFISH with hypnotic powers and a mind of his own. When his owner Tom takes him on a trip to the seaside, he finds himself in a stand-off with a Super Zombie Eel – has the fierce fish finally met his match? In the second story, all eyes are on Frankie as he takes on a starring role in the school play!

FRANKIE'S BACK, AND THIS TIME IT'S PERSONAL!

Frankie is a BIG FAT ZOMBIE GOLDFISH with hypnotic powers. When his owner Tom takes him camping, something fishy starts going on. Could the zombie fish finally have met his match? In story two, Frankie's been kidnapped! Can Tom rescue his fishy friend before it's too late?

VISIT THE GOBSTOPPERS WEBSITE FOR

AUTHOR NEWS · BONUS CONTENT
VIDEOS · GAMES · PRIZES . . .

AND MORE!